"In literature as in music, addressing topics directly isn't Ribot's way . . . As a sideman—with Tom Waits, Elvis Costello, Marianne Faithfull, Yoko Ono, Arto Lindsay, James Carter, Susana Baca, the Jazz Passengers, and his musical soul mate John Zorn, among countless others—he's always aimed to be direct and disruptive simultaneously, and the same goes for his writing."   —Robert Christgau, *And It Don't Stop*

"In the beginning, we may have thought Marc Ribot was a full-time Lower East Side tenants rights activist who moonlit as an ubiquitous downtown noise guitarist. Now we come to find out he's a phenomenal essay writer who has the nerve to be one of our loudest and most beloved electric jazz improvisers . . . Ribot mostly composes essays about music and life of sublime wit, probity, and severe self-reckoning, as well as some quite absurdist fiction and film (mis)treatments . . . Finally, we submit, do you know anyone else who's written a laugh-out-loud funny tale about an angry wife who murders her husband after Botox plasters over her menacing glare? No, you certainly do not."

—Greg Tate, author of *Everything But the Burden*

"*Unstrung* . . . delivers everything one could hope from a guitar hero/activist/cultural critic: that is, complex culture and musical theory broken down into tasteful riffs, absurdist tales of our times, and plenty of sparse, unpretentious prose as well-honed as any major American writer."   —*BOMB Magazine*

"Ribot is not only a gifted musician but also a talented wordsmith, and this quirky volume will appeal to music aficionados who appreciate strong writing with observational, intelligent, and provocative themes."   —*Library Journal*

"*Unstrung* has all the honesty, original angles, beauty, and clangor found in Marc Ribot's playing. His compassionate writing about Frantz Casseus gives a human face to his calls for artists' rights. Like life itself, this book is bloody, funny, and bloody funny."   —Elvis Costello, musician

"An insightful tour through the razor-sharp mind of one of the world's most original and influential guitar masters. Ribot's acerbic wit, self-deprecating humor, and profoundly vexing love-hate relationship with all things guitar make for a fun and stimulating read."   —John Zorn, musician

"Don't let the fact that I am calling Marc Ribot a thinking musician distract from the raw and the righteous aspects of his playing and of this book. You have to love something completely to want to look for a way out. Here is more proof of Marc's love and understanding of music, of those who make it and of all the imaginings that it might jar loose!"   —Arto Lindsay, musician

"*Unstrung* is proof that the iconoclast Marc Ribot has a way with words commensurate with his guitar virtuosity . . . Ribot's is the voice of an outsider breaking through. It's the voice of an original."   —*Pittsburgh Post-Gazette*

"Ribot . . . produced a book that is much like his musical output: difficult to categorize but fascinating and engaging."
                                                          —*Inside Hook*

"Ribot is a keen observer of the irresolvable tension between creativity and commerce."   —*New York City Jazz Record*

"This is [Ribot's] first book and it's a mix of music writing and short fiction. Marc has a wicked smart sense of humor and isn't shy to talk about his strong political leanings. And you can bet that he'll crank it up to 11!"   —*Book Musik*

MARC RIBOT has released twenty-five albums under his own name over a forty-year career, exploring everything from the pioneering jazz of Albert Ayler to the Cuban *son* of Arsenio Rodríguez. *Rolling Stone* points out that "Ribot helped Tom Waits refine a new, weird Americana on 1985's *Rain Dogs*, and since then he's become the go-to guitar guy for all kinds of roots-music adventurers: Robert Plant and Alison Krauss, Elvis Costello, John Mellencamp." Additional recording credits include Neko Case, Diana Krall, Elton John/Leon Russell's *The Union*, Solomon Burke, John Lurie's Lounge Lizards, Marianne Faithfull, Joe Henry, Allen Toussaint, Medeski, Martin & Wood, Caetano Veloso, Allen Ginsberg, Madeleine Peyroux, Norah Jones, the Black Keys, and many others. Ribot works regularly with Grammy Award–winning producer T Bone Burnett and New York composer John Zorn. He has also performed on numerous film scores such as *Walk the Line, The Kids Are All Right,* and *The Departed.*

RANTS AND STORIES

Unstrung

OF A NOISE GUITARIST

RANTS AND STORIES

Unstrung

OF A NOISE GUITARIST

MARC RIBOT

BROOKLYN, NEW YORK

Published by Akashic Books
©2021 Marc Ribot

The lyrics included on page 98 are excerpted from "Like a Rolling Stone" by Bob Dylan.

Paperback ISBN: 978-1-63614-067-4
Hardcover ISBN: 978-1-61775-930-7
Library of Congress Control Number: 2020948049

All rights reserved
First paperback printing

Akashic Books
Brooklyn, New York
Instagram, Twitter, Facebook: AkashicBooks
E-mail: info@akashicbooks.com
Website: www.akashicbooks.com

Table of Contents

Introduction:
Ribot the Writer
by Lynne Tillman

Friends call him Ribot.

Like-minded musicians will instantly respond to Ribot's stance on playing LOUD, announced in *Unstrung* in the first section, "Lies and Distortion." Ribot writes: "I'm a guitarist who points extremely loud amplifiers directly at his head." He wants musicians using "distorted sounds . . . to plac[e] their amps at risk." What this risk means to him, I can't elucidate, but it is essential to his music.

Ribot is an extremist, intense in all things.

His distinction between "lies and distortion"—musical distortion also—is telling. No matter what subject he writes about, Ribot will also present shades of himself, his ideas, his memories. As an unreliable narrator, he cautions his readers: do not expect the impossible, absolute Truth, but proximate and fictional truths.

Like all human beings, he lives with contradictions.

Ribot's stories and essays show his fierce attachment to music, which joins with his anarchistic and passionate spirit. He maintains a devoted if complicated relationship to Judaism, a rage against capitalism, and a lifelong advocacy for human rights and musicians' rights. Ribot writes of fatal mistakes, is sometimes melancholic, and reckons with futility.

His belief in justice is as strong as his belief in the greatness of the late guitarist Robert Quine. An eponymous essay showcases Quine's broad knowledge of music history, while Ribot catalogs their friendship, his respect for and love of Quine. "We mostly talked about guitar equipment . . . But guitar equipment, for those who love it, is a language." That kind of love runs through Ribot's pieces. Nothing exists here that doesn't carry it.

He cannily converts musical ideas, a wordless language with its own vocabulary, into words. "The line Quine traced through history, the qualities he looked for in used guitars and fuzz boxes, were those with the force of being to cut a wound in the numb skin of pop." *The numb skin of pop* kills me. Language also moves him.

Ribot credits his mentors, remembers their glory, and mourns them. He memorializes bassist Henry Grimes, who played in one of Ribot's bands not long before he died. Ribot's essays on classical guitarist/composer Frantz Casseus, his mentor on the guitar, and musician/producer/entrepreneur Hal Willner are elegiacal. Ribot elucidates who Willner was, what he did, and makes his death, his loss to music and more, tragic.

Ribot tells an old story about Casseus. It's the one about how composers and musicians get screwed by the music industry. Casseus was sick and old, living in a nursing home, on Medicaid, when money owed him forever finally arrived. Money never was the reason Casseus played and composed, but "holding the delayed check [for $16,000] in his one good hand," Ribot writes, Casseus said to him, "If I had known, I would have composed more. I felt my work to be without value."

Ribot's essay on "Time" explains his discovery that, in transcribing tapes for Ivorian griot Emile Yoan's band, the result on the sheet was different rhythmically from the group's sound. Some years later, playing in Susana Baca's group, he realized he "had been completely mishearing where 'one' was . . . the aural signs which allow the listener to distinguish one from three, upbeat from downbeat, are culturally determined." It's true in all languages, and, in a written language, tone and rhythm are built from a complex arrangement of words, which produces meanings.

His acute and tender fictions move from old loves— "'Meet you downstairs' was code meaning he didn't want to sleep with her"—to new ones, new hopes, and sorrows. Ribot exposes his vulnerability and doubts, willfully. His fine ear pushes him to write stories based on sound, on hearing, unlike any I know.

In "We Tell Children the Cow Says Moo," he recounts reading to his little daughter: ". . . the rooster [says] 'cock-a-doodle-do.'" This "truth" drives Ribot to listen hard to an actual rooster's call: "As it turns out," he writes, "roosters don't say 'cock-a-doodle do' . . . instead they emit a strange scream, punctuated into roughly three sections . . ."

His fictions survey the human comedy—disappointments; the American dream turned horror movie; people losing their minds or never finding themselves, and people defeated by society's rigors and condemnations. His rhythms hit where they should.

His on-and-off-the-road stories are dedicated to honesty. "O Say Can You See" opens with these sentences: "American life is lonely. I call you sometimes, when I'm off the road. We have coffee near your stop on the N train. The trains are slower now. Most often, I don't call." Loneliness is personified in these lines.

Over the years, knowing Ribot since the 1980s, I have watched and heard him play many times, and close up. He holds his guitar close to his body, and, generally, drops his head, almost on his instrument. He's so bent over, you can't see the guitar, so he and his guitar merge, form a new body, alive in its own world, where he wants to be. He doesn't want to see us, because he plays as much, maybe more, to hear what he's doing as he does to be heard by an audience.

Ribot writes with great care for words, for sounds. It means as much to him to get it right, and be true to it, as to his music. A good writer, like a good musician, and Ribot is both, needs to know what they're composing to be able to understand it, maybe even do it better the next time.

Marc Ribot's stories are moving and compassionate. They are revelatory, honest, and insightful, but see for yourself, and read them.

Lynne Tillman is a novelist, short story writer, and essayist. Her most recent novels are *American Genius, A Comedy* and *Men and Apparitions*. The latest short story collection, *The Complete Madame Realism and Other Stories*, was published by Semiotext(e). In 2022, an autobiographical, book-length essay, *Mothercare*, will be published by Soft Skull, and the following year, a collection of Tillman's short stories. She lives in New York with bass player David Hofstra.

Part I

LIES AND DISTORTION

Lies and Distortion

Hi. My name is Marc. I'm a guitarist who points extremely loud amplifiers directly at his head. Very often. Sometimes as often as two hundred nights a year for the past forty-five years. Audiologists say this could make one's ears howl, create an uncomfortable sensation of density in one's head, and eventually make it impossible to hear human conversation. Yet I persist . . . Why?

It's true most amps sound better at volumes loud enough to fray the edge of notes with the subtle distortion that is to electric guitars what makeup is to a drag queen of a certain age. Not accidentally, as manufacturers in the late '50s and early '60s raced to design equipment with less and less distortion, guitarists turned up louder and louder to subvert their efforts. Nor are guitarists alone in this desire to strain.

We seem to love broken voices in general: vocal cords eroded by whiskey and screaming, the junked-out weakness of certain horn players, distortion which signifies surpassing the capabilities of a tube or a speaker—voices that distort, damage, but (at least in performance) don't actually die. The singer pushes through the note, the horn player eventually finds breath, the amplifier struggles on but doesn't explode and become silent.

Was this always true? I don't know. Maybe it means something that representation of the struggle (once shown by the trembling effect called *vibrato*) to maintain the distance necessary to hold an instrument or sing a note in the face of overwhelming emotion is signified in our time by a direct attack on the equipment itself. True vibrato sounds old-fashioned to us; think of Django Reinhardt's guitar sound, Caruso's voice, the saxophone in Guy Lombardo's band. Somewhere along the line an inflation occurred in the currency of pain, and the price of our musical fix was more than mere notes could carry.

Another term for distortion is low-fidelity. Maybe we distrust our voices and that's why we're unfaithful to them. Beginning in the mid-to-late '60s, producers of guitar equipment began to recognize our need to be unfaithful by making equipment designed to produce distortion. Some amps had little knobs on them that said *distortion*, with numbers from one to ten. Although the public at first confused guitarists who fell for this maneuver with creators of genuine damage such as Jimi Hendrix, the sounds produced soon became completely predictable.

My chief complaint against some practitioners of heavy metal guitar from the early '70s through the early '80s is that I can immediately tell their distorted sounds are not really placing their amps at risk. To whatever extent I have a moral sensibility, this offends it. I much prefer the subtler but less predictable distortions of the '40s and '50s (e.g., Charlie Christian, Hubert Sumlin, Pee Wee Crayton, Ike Turner, Chuck Berry),[1] a time when amp designers weren't

---

1 It's not that I'm nostalgic—contemporary inheritors of this tradition of sonic risk include Robert Quine, James Blood Ulmer, and legions of others more or less influenced by some or all of the above.

such wiseasses. Still, the total deafness of those metal guitarists to these considerations lends them a certain charm all their own.

The astute reader may point out that a smaller amplifier would produce the proper ratio of "clean" signal to distortion at a lower volume. True. Also true: I have often used Marshall half stacks—large, loud amps. This was because I wanted to preserve at all costs the option of playing with a partially distorted sound—using a larger amp turned up almost all the way—rather than be trapped with the overdistorted sound (produced by having a smaller amp up all the way) typical of late-'60s white blues players.

If subtle distortion is makeup, the heavy, homogenous distortion of these guitarists (Eric Clapton, in a phrase demeaning to women everywhere, referred to his sound at the time as "woman tone") amounts to a type of airbrushing. This is especially true when it is used in conjunction with the type of grandiose large-room reverbs and echoes supplying every amplified squirt in a garage band with the imaginary ambience of the Milan Central train station. It is the sonic equivalent of Fascist architecture. The effect (and probably the intent) is to eliminate the little clicks and imperfections that belie the god-stature of the guitar hero and to give the impression that the guitar is a strong, bellowing voice rather than a frame for frail pieces of metal whose vibrations soon die.

All guitarists fight this death, this logarithmic decline into silence, and its implied presence in every note may be one of the reasons guitars (more than bowed or wind instruments, whose notes can be sustained at will) have long been linked to sadness and despair. Guitar is the essential instrument of blues. Picasso chose it to accompany images of death during his "blue" period. The best-known piece from the first famous guitar virtuoso, John Dowland (sixteenth-century English), is titled "John Dowland Is Always Sad" (*"Semper Dowland, Semper Dolens"*).

Some guitarists fight it by squeezing the last bit out of a note with vibrato. Others use the mandolin technique of picking many notes very fast, hoping no one will notice (the best-known example being Francisco Tárrega's "Recuerdos de la Alhambra"). Volume also works. The sound from the amp reinforces the vibrations of the strings, creating increasingly longer sustains up to the point of feedback. Still, to struggle with the decay and death of notes (in music, things decay before they die) is one thing. To try to actually win seems somehow wrong: a Faustian error. Hence the Marshall half stack.

I know. All the above is at best a limited explanation for years of nightly volume abuse. Those with a Freudian orientation might by now be tempted to see this preference for large amplifiers and loud sounds as a type of . . . compensation.

Dear reader, let me assure you—nothing could be further from the truth. Still, the ghosts of early musical traumas do hover above the volume knobs, urging me to acts of excess as surely as Grandma's memories of childhood deprivation kept pulling her back to the refrigerator long after her stomach was full.

The experiences in question are of a type rarely described by music critics, yet so obvious to musicians as to be practically nameless. As soon as I started playing in public, I began to experience the struggle between the "power" of my amp (then a lovely Ampeg B-12) and the social and economic power of bandleaders, club owners, paying members of the audience, band members, etc.: the ones Sartre was talking about when he said, "Hell is other people."

Critics tend to write about the material conditions of music-making as if they were a neutral garden in which little artistic seedlings, fertilized perhaps by the critic's own careful attentions, grow slowly toward the light of aesthetic beauty. Nice Marxist critics may believe the conception of aesthetic beauty has something to do with the economy, but all seem agreed on the first point. What's missing from this perspective is an understanding of social constraints: having sublime moments interrupted by enraged diners who can't talk over their shrimp boats, enduring the harsh complaints of newlyweds who feel your style is spoiling their blessed event, and of being subjected to professional criticism itself: although most critics see themselves as observers outside the process, musicians see them as part of a power structure, albeit the least powerful part, not significantly different from the preceding examples. (This disjunction in perspectives may be why the reaction of many musicians on first seeing their work reviewed is uncontrollable laughter, followed by a faint nausea and a feeling of being misunderstood which will, if they are lucky, last their whole lives.)

The relation between amp wattage and social power can be even stickier within bands, those little units which invariably replicate the most dysfunctional elements of their members' families. What guitarist has not had to endure horrible meetings in which electronically deprived members of the band (drummers, sax players, vocalists) attempt to reason with them, appealing to a sense of compassion and egalitarianism usually altogether lacking in their own rock 'n' roll will-to-power personas, or, that failing, resorting to threats or brute force? This banal scenario is a usually doomed attempt to check the famous "dialectic of rock and roll," which can be heard played out on many a stage nightly: you turn up, so I turn up, so you turn up . . . etc.

Technology being advanced as it is, the only possible end point of this escalation is the limit of human endurance. And here is where distortion/volume as a metaphor meets the medical phenomenon.

When acoustic pain occurs in the theater of rock (and judging by those hilarious clips from decades past, almost every one of its mutations has been initially felt as brutal or painful, no matter how benign they sound to later ears), the pain of the audience is compensated by their pleasure at the spectacle of the sacrifice of the musicians, who, since they are standing closer to the amps, are theoretically experiencing even greater and more destructive pain. In fact, mammoth sound systems in the hands of deaf or sadistic sound persons often make the room volume louder than the stage volume, but this only heightens the theatrical effect. In this illusion, the musician is both sacrificial victim and magical protector who filters the dangerous volume levels through his/her body (literally standing between amp and audience) to protect the audience, in a ritual not unlike how shamans filter strong poisons through their bodies so that others can enjoy the less toxic residue by drinking their hallucinogenic piss. In a reversal of StarKist Tuna priorities, rock audiences are more than willing to suffer bitter acoustic phenomena in order to achieve ritual/aesthetic satisfaction. Thanks, Charlie.

I don't know how they do the trick with the poison mushrooms, but the truth about playing really loud is this: on a really good night, nothing hurts—not howling volume, not airless rooms at sauna temperatures, not bleeding callouses, not a fever of 103, not a bottle in the head, not a recent divorce. Nothing much. Not till later.

So—the unresolved social conflicts of the band are translated by ever louder sound systems into a theater of pain for the audience, and everyone goes home happy. But the shamans are cheating. They are going deaf or using earplugs, enabling them to avoid indefinitely the consequences of intraband social failure, and violating the shamanistic pact with the audience—feeding them the poison undiluted. The audience, of course, senses this deception and begins to go deaf or use earplugs themselves, degrading the entire spectacle (and necessitating/giving birth to alternate theatrical forms such as stage diving). The bands in turn sense their lapse in shamanic power and crank it up still louder . . .

Oh my. Where will it all end? If the birth of symphony orchestras foreshadowed the arrival of parliamentary government, and the Beatles prefigured the hippie commune, one can only imagine what post-Bosnian nightmare or total failure of language is lurking noisily in our futures, blocked out/symbolized/invited by the earplugs I wore at the gig last night. Don't blame me: doctor's orders.

Guitars

My relation with the guitar is one of struggle—I'm constantly forcing it to be something else: a saxophone, a scream, a cart rolling down a hill. Sometimes it obeys. Sometimes I give up and play surf music (what all electric guitars want to play). Surf music's okay, for a while. Then something always comes up that needs translation, and there we go again . . . Guitars don't mind struggle. Guitars *are* struggle. Classical guitars aren't built in that wavy shape only to imitate the bodies of women (although it's a lovely shape), but precisely because wavy isn't the natural shape of straight grained wood. Bending the wood, then binding it together in this unnatural shape, gives guitars the tension that creates their resonance.

A guitar is a kind of wooden spring. Serious classical guitarists prefer guitars under twenty years old. After that, they lose the tension that makes them beautiful.

I often think of guitars abandoned in closets, silent constructions against the memory of the wood, a resistance, like Atlas's, noticed only when it fails. Rock and postrock solid-body guitars, at least those not shaped like V's or teardrops, only mimic this shape, and don't strain against themselves in this very literal way—which may be why the sense of tension became transformed into the aesthetic content of the material being performed, or into the bodies of the performers, who now, inexplicably, feel the need to stand up. In any case, I've lived with guitars a long time. I've bent them. And they've bent me.

Frantz Casseus

In 1965, at age eleven, I wanted to play guitar: like millions of other suburban kids, I heard a Rolling Stones record and thought it was cool. I had no interest in classical guitar. Yet that's what I started studying, with no less a teacher than Frantz Casseus, the acknowledged father of Haitian classical guitar. And although I wound up playing music quite far from what Frantz taught me, it was a good idea, a beautiful idea in fact, for reasons that don't make any kind of sense but are true.

I'd known Frantz most of my life. He'd been friends with my aunt and uncle, Rhoda and Melvin Unger, since the early '50s, eventually forming one of those unlikely re-invented families that seem to grow out of the social fragments of New York life. My aunt and uncle both attended the famously leftist City College of the 1930s, met shortly thereafter, and have been together ever since. By the time they met Frantz, my aunt had become a pop songwriter and my uncle was running a costume jewelry business in the Garment District.

Frantz was born in Port-au-Prince, Haiti, in 1915. His childhood fascination with the guitar was mystically fused with the death of a young aunt who had helped raise him. It was the custom in Haiti to discard the belongings of those who died from illness. ("The sight of [Aunt Andrée's] mandolin perched on what seemed a pile of garbage—alongside the memory of her music—has never ceased to haunt me . . . I burned with desire.")[2] By the time he emigrated to New York, Frantz had already established himself as an important guitarist in Port-au-Prince cultural circles. But he had ambitions beyond the repetition of a traditional classical repertoire for Haiti's cultural elite.

Frantz came to New York for roughly the same reasons James Baldwin left it. Both needed to write about the place they were from and both needed to leave that place in order to do so. Frantz came here with the ambition to compose a distinctly Haitian classical guitar music, to fuse the European classical tradition with Haitian folk elements, as Heitor Villa-Lobos had done with his native Brazil's and as Béla Bartók had done with Hungarian folk songs.

Frantz's assumption of what was to be a lifelong musical mission followed the occupation of Haiti by the US military (1915–1934), when its cultural integrity must have felt threatened. An editorial he wrote titled "Our Méringue Is Dying" describes this: "Some with indifference, others with an indignant sadness, have witnessed the disappearance of one of our most delicious national dances which is like a precious pearl ornament of our folklore." The Haitian Méringue "invites [one] to dance, contains a subtle and delicious melody . . . [Its] character, its simple and limited form, made it a dance with noble stature, and even a

2 Marc Methalier, ed., *Essai Bibliographique sur la Vie de Frantz Casseus* (Port-au-Prince, Haiti: Mathel Productions, 1995).

classic."[3] Love and loss again, this time on a national/cultural level.

Frantz's artistic reaction to this perceived loss, his "indignant sadness," occurred against a backdrop in which the Haitian classical guitar repertoire was completely determined by what was being performed in Europe. Frantz looked instead to Haitian folk forms: "I believe it is the artist's function to render articulately and with beauty the soul of the land of his origin and also the world that he experiences . . . As you may know, my work is considered an expression of the Haitian spirit. Yet, critics have stated (and this has been my hope) that it transcends regionalism and enters the realm of transnational art."[4]

This leap of imagination may seem obvious from a contemporary standpoint, but in the Haiti of the late '30s and early '40s it was anything but. Aimé Césaire was only just articulating the negritude movement. To imagine a fusion of the European classical tradition and Haitian folk music, to imagine the "Haitian spirit" as relevant and necessary to "the realm of transnational art," was bold and shocking.

Before Frantz could incorporate Haitian folklore into the tradition of the classical guitar, he first had to study it. As the relatively protected son of a civil servant (his father headed the Department of Water Supply), Frantz had had limited direct experience of Haitian folk culture. He dropped out of law school in order to become a full-time guitarist. He then set out to make contacts "with certain griots and people initiated in our culture. Thus strength-

---

3 Frantz Casseus, "Notre Méringue se muert," *Haiti Journal*, 1944.
4 Interview with Ira Landgarten, *Frets Magazine* #17, 1989.

ened, I overflowed with rhythms, forms, lyrics of my future compositions."

Frantz's relation with the US occupiers was complex. He'd heard jazz on the soldiers' radios and phonographs. Although his sense of musical mission emerged from a desire to protect Haitian music from this cultural intrusion, he was also attracted to jazz. Frantz told me he had wanted to come to New York to meet Fats Waller. The meeting never took place; Waller had already died by the time Frantz arrived in 1946. But the influence is audible in Frantz's stride piano/jazz harmony–inflected composition "Romance" and was visible in his appreciation of well-made hats. Frantz initially stayed at the Sloane YMCA and various Upper West Side addresses before settling at 312 West 87th Street, where he completed *Haitian Suite*, the masterpiece he recorded in 1954 for Folkways Records (whose catalog has been reissued by Smithsonian).

In time, Frantz and my uncle and aunt became friends, hung out, and eventually had a sort of cooperative arrangement regarding a car. As a kid, I used to come in from New Jersey with my family to visit my aunt and uncle on West 86th Street. Frantz would be there, and we'd spend Saturday or Sunday together. Every Thanksgiving and Passover, Frantz would be with us, whether in New Jersey or New York. Sometimes he'd bring his guitar and play. He was the first person I ever heard play a musical instrument live. When I decided to study guitar, it was decided that I would study with him.

I would arrive for my lessons at Frantz's brownstone every Sunday afternoon at one. Often, to my amazement, Frantz would still be sleeping. The apartment smelled of black coffee, stained wood, and cigarettes. The place resembled an assemblage inspired by cubist painting. Frantz was a skilled woodworker and luthier—during his life, he hand-made more than 150 guitars to supplement his income. Every week would bring some alteration to the maze of cabinets and bookshelves.

While Frantz got dressed, I'd sit and warm up on the guitar. I could see, on the coffee table, artifacts of the night before: manuscript paper, pencils, and the ashes of entire cigarettes, ten or more, maybe puffed once or twice then left in the ashtray to burn out untouched and forgotten. The story of someone composing, someone lost in the solitude of music.

Frantz was a patient teacher, and in fact, much of what is taught in the study of classical guitar is patience itself. The counterintuitive ability to relax the hands instead of tensing them before the difficult task of playing, the secret that impossible physical feats become possible if broken up into tiny components and approached very, very slowly.

I stopped studying with Frantz at age fourteen and started playing in rock bands. I moved to Boston, then to Maine. Somewhere along the line, I became a musician. I moved to New York in 1977, crashed in my aunt and uncle's spare bedroom for a few months, then moved downtown and lived my life.

What did Frantz do? To quote from the Tuscany Publications book of Frantz's works for solo guitar: "In the late '60s Casseus began to compose again for voice and guitar, publishing the album *Haitienesques*. In 1969, he released the recording *Haitiana* on the Afro-Carib label (now available on CD through Smithsonian Folkways as *Haitian Dances, Haitian Suite*).

"Although Casseus continued to compose through the 1980s, his career as a performing guitarist was hampered from 1970 onward by an increasingly debilitating tendon problem in his left hand. This eventually forced a premature retirement from concertizing, which, combined with the unavailability of his recordings, contributed to a loss of Casseus's visibility on the US classical guitar scene. Afro-Carib had gone out of business and Folkways was highly disorganized in its later years."

I noticed Frantz's increasing difficulties only gradually, from the distance I'd placed between my family and myself. At that time, I felt my studies with Frantz had been at best a quaint diversion from the electric path my music had taken. At worst, I cursed the frustrating right-hand slowness of execution resulting from my failed fifteen-year attempt to play electric guitar classical style, without a pick. It was only beginning to dawn on me that the economy forced on me by that slowness had been my aesthetic salvation, the frustration itself a connection to a frustrated no-wave musical moment.

I was plucked from my self-absorption by a phone call from Rhoda: Frantz was in trouble. For years, he'd been in a state of denial about the increasing clumsiness of his left hand. Current medical expertise would most likely have recommended a respite from playing. At the time, Frantz thought that he just needed to practice more. But the more he practiced, the clumsier he got, till he could hardly play at all. He believed, had to believe, that he was making progress. Eventually his delusion collided with the world: Frantz accepted a concert engagement in honor of his contributions to Haitian culture from the Société de recherche et de diffusion de la musique Haïtienne in Montreal.

My aunt's plan, seemingly stolen from one of the musical comedy scripts she'd pitched (and sold) to Broadway producers, was for me to act as the unofficial understudy in case things went badly. I'd already learned some of Frantz's pieces as his student; I started practicing the rest. Frantz took off for Montreal about five days before the concert. On day three, Rhoda, who had somehow made herself available to the concert promoters, began to receive calls of increasing urgency. I got on a plane to Montreal and stayed up most of that night with Frantz, correcting my interpretation of his pieces. The next evening, after having survived an early-morning audition before representatives of the Société, I played Frantz's repertoire in concert.

It wasn't a brilliant concert—classical guitarist is one of those jobs, like professional football linebacker, in which one doesn't dabble—but it was okay. My relief was tempered with regret; it wasn't quite right that by default I had wound up as Frantz's main interpreter. And I was concerned over what Frantz must actually have felt as he accepted the audience's applause.

Back in New York, Frantz's tendon problems, in spite (or because) of an operation on his wrist and other medical interventions, didn't improve. Another composer might have shifted to piano as a tool and continued writing. But Frantz's attachment to music was through the guitar. "Of all musical instruments, classical guitar is closest to the human voice," Frantz liked to say. In no way, of course, is this objectively true, but it was true for Frantz; it was *his* human voice.

There was another source of discouragement: he wasn't

receiving much income from what he'd written. The work was generating income: his vocal version of "Merci Bon Dieu," one of the *Haitian Suite* pieces, had been recorded by Harry Belafonte, French vocalist Gilles Dreu, and others. But Frantz was the victim of a classic music-biz malaise. He had, over the course of his career, signed publishing deals with various companies that had been sold and resold. My mother, Harriet Ribot, had offered to help Frantz untangle this knot in order to both generate income for him and clear the rights to publish Frantz's work in book form. The process took over a decade.

A series of strokes and heart attacks left Frantz increasingly debilitated during his last years. We were in close touch during that time—Frantz supervised my recording of his solo guitar pieces for the Disques du Crépuscule label from his 87th Street nursing-home bed. Although paralyzed in half his body and often finding it difficult to form words, Frantz was mentally alert and able to make insightful critiques of the work. During this period Frantz was visited by friends, family, and well-wishers from the Haitian cultural scene, where his status as a major composer is well established. In 1992 he was honored as "a living testimony of Haitian cultural survival with authenticity" by the Recreational, Artistic and Literary Haitian Club of New York. In Haiti itself, bootlegs of Frantz's recordings are still circulated.

Frantz Casseus did what he'd set out from Haiti to do. In order to do it, he chose a life of great solitude, imposed on himself a type of exile, forfeited (although he was by no means celibate) the pleasures of a wife and children, spent his life on the edge of poverty, and lived as a Black man in a United States whose Southern racists wouldn't let him stay in the hotels where he performed and whose Northern liberals had difficulty accepting his work as classical, preferring to hear it within a "folk" context when they heard it at all. He carried these burdens with such little complaint they seemed not to matter. Those who knew Frantz knew better. But Frantz chose this life because he loved composing, he loved playing the classical guitar. Love's burdens are lightly borne. Frantz died in June 1993. Before he did, my aunt, my mother, and I promised him that we'd look after his work. The first print book of Frantz Casseus's complete works for solo classical guitar, *Frantz Casseus: Guitar Works,* was released in 2003 by Tuscany Publications and is available now through Schott Music (ECH1721).

Horn Section

In Maine, from 1974 to 1978, I eventually drifted into gigs with a few of the Black musicians working that not-very-hospitable-to-R&B circuit. First was Fred Williams (name changed), against whose dislocated Jimmy Smith I played my very best fake Wes Montgomery, Grant Green, or Cornell Dupree. Actually, Fred had more in common with the many New Jersey/New York imitators who attempted to glaze some layer of funky jazz signification over the Top 40 repertoire demanded of lounge bands than with Jimmy Smith, Jack McDuff, Jimmy McGriff, Groove Holmes, or the other geniuses of the Hammond B3.

Although Fred never made that A-list, he'd come up on a neighboring circuit, playing four or five sets a night on stages built atop elevated islands in the middle of circular bars—a cultural phenomenon that seemed to cross race and class lines in mid-'70s New Jersey's lounge world.

Williams had imported the social traditions of the New Jersey lounge musicians as well, the time-honored response to the boredom of the breaks between the nightly sets. I remember one of several pieces of wisdom Fred imparted: "Always eat some really greasy food *before* you start drinking . . . coats the stomach." In that way, Fred hoped to avoid getting as drunk as the women he was drinking with, thus affording himself a tactical advantage later on, when relative sobriety was helpful in the delicate task of transferring the night's catch from barstool to bedroom (or at least automobile).

While such Newark folkways dovetailed well enough with those of many of Augusta's working-class lounge dwellers, they created a kind of cognitive dissonance with the granola-flecked feminism of some of the hippier refugees from Boston or NYC—my girlfriend Micki among them. Micki and I were on the poorer end of the hippie urban refugee bell curve: we had aimed to go "back to the land" but had miscalculated slightly (by forgetting, for example, to have the money to buy land), and wound up in a tenement apartment in Augusta, a wooden firetrap whose sole source of heat was kerosene canisters lugged up four flights of outdoor back stairway, and poured into a stove/heater. This demanded frequent feedings during the cold weather (i.e., from late September through mid-May), and would, unless primed perfectly, send dangerous flames shooting up to the ceiling.

Anyway, the year was 1976, which I believe would still be counted as the Thermidor of second-wave feminism. Eager to put her recently acquired theoretical background to work, Micki (short for Mary Magdalene) seized on Fred's rather sad attempts at womanizing as proof that he was the very patriarch Susan Brownmiller had warned us about. And so, untroubled in her righteous anger by the hint of racism that the statistical unlikelihood of her choosing Fred to represent the sexist impulses of the male population of Maine might have suggested, she leapt into the fray. Refusing to allow our happy home to be the alibi Fred had requested, Micki instead phoned Fred's long-suffering wife to tell her exactly what she believed to be "the truth" about his location till three a.m. the previous evening.

Much unpleasantness ensued, and nobody involved wound up on good terms. I did a few more lounge appearances with Fred, but he soon landed a steady gig with a Connecticut-based Top 40 band, and split. His wife recovered quickly, though, locating a new and even more reliable supplier of suffering within a few weeks of his departure.

We were plentiful in the Augusta of the mid-1970s.

Later, I subbed for the regular guitarist in a Lewiston-based quartet covering classic '60s soul/blues/R&B: Sam & Dave, B.B. King, James Brown (and his Famous Flames).

I don't remember the name of the band, or any of the individual musicians' names.

What I do remember is this: it was my first time playing with a horn section, and the experience of soloing call-and-response against an R&B horn section remains one of the most powerful and joyful things I've ever known.

One might well ask what kind of horn section a quartet, one of whose members was a twenty-one-year-old substitute guitarist, could manage—but this quartet provided a creative answer: the drummer managed to accompany the tenor sax by playing trumpet with his right hand, while still nailing the snare beats with his left.

It wasn't fancy, but they were tight, and it did the trick, letting my solos float upward, propelled by the steady blasts below, each repetition of the horn line both dialogue and affirmation: like a strong wind at your back as you run the last lap of a race. Although I'm sure my inexperience was obvious to all—I'd started out on classical guitar, hadn't yet learned to play with a pick, and my knowledge of the tunes was missing a bridge or two—I instantly felt like I was home. I don't know if the older musicians recognized something too . . . anyway, they were nice, tolerant guys.

During a break, the drummer told me that he had perfected his one-handed trumpet technique while playing in circuses touring the South—they had played fourteen-hour shifts with no break, from ten a.m. till midnight every day. The musicians had to spell each other in order to eat and go to the toilet. As it turned out, he'd played a little trumpet in high school. And as the trumpet player on the gig was a passable drummer, an alliance of convenience and survival was formed, and a skill, born in the sweaty tents of South Carolina and Georgia, became audible in the chillier bars of Maine.

I think of that story sometimes now, of how thin the veil is, in time and circumstance, that separates us from the historic condition of musicians—since time immemorial associated with hard times, beggary, and prostitution.

To whatever extent "professional" status was ever a reality for most of my colleagues, it was a function of the extension of copyright to sound recordings at the beginning of the twentieth century, and the power of the American Federation of Musicians pre–Taft-Hartley law.

The union's power today is, outside a few elites, mostly vestigial.

And copyright is under attack by ad-based online platforms with more money than god. The math that brought down the record industry is simple: the lower the cost of content, the more clicks, the higher the ad rates, the bigger the profits.

It took some musicians awhile to figure out that this game was rigged against us—but math never was our collective strong point.

Robert Quine

Robert Quine, former guitarist with Richard Hell & the Voidoids, Lou Reed, and many others—inconsolable since the death of his wife Alice a year earlier—killed himself in May 2004 at the age of sixty-one. Quine pioneered the sound of punk rock guitar soloing. Listen to his work on Lou Reed's "Waves of Fear," or with Richard Hell & the Voidoids: Malcolm McLaren heard the Voidoids on their first UK tour and soon after formed the Sex Pistols.

Quine was an obsessive record collector with an encyclopedic knowledge of rock, blues, and jazz. He once made me a cassette of rare Ike Turner tracks from the '50s. On it, Turner, playing a (newly invented) Stratocaster Tremolo bar guitar, takes this insane solo, completely noise/punk. Robert copied the solo three times on my cassette just in case I missed it. This is almost all you need to know about rock history: it has never belonged to the people who play it right.

It may seem odd to punk-identified fans that Quine, who never played a single jazz lick, practiced hours a day along with bebop records. (What I wouldn't give to hear what Quine, alone in his studio, actually did play over his Barney Kessel or Johnny Smith records.) It seems less odd to musicians that Quine could trace a line through Blind Willie Johnson, Lester Young, Albert Ayler, Ike Turner, the Velvet Underground, and extend it into what became "punk."

In a *New York Magazine* eulogy called "Delicate Rage," Richard Hell describes Quine's own solos as "perfectly structured but outrageously wild expositions," and writes that Quine was a "connoisseur of moronic rapture." What ties the contradictory sides of Hell's description together is the idea of critique: pushing self-expression to the breaking point of noise/wildness problematizes it. Pushing formalist constraint to the point of the moronic/autistic problematizes it. (Check out Quine and Fred Maher's *Basic* in which the rhythm section's "basic tracks," normally completed by the addition/overdubbing of the featured vocalist and soloists, are instead presented as a minimalist finished masterpiece.)

Quine and I got along because we never talked about stuff like this. We mostly talked about guitar equipment. He once insisted I accompany him to Manny's on 48th Street to try out the "Buzz Box," a particularly horrible distortion pedal. The box's black metal covering was painted in drips of yellow paint to simulate strands of vomit. I bought it instantly, and it was a point of pride with Robert, after Manny's discontinued selling the Buzz Box, that the store had sold only three of them: to him, to me, and to another customer who had sent it back assuming it to be defective.

But guitar equipment, for those who love it, is a language. The line Quine traced through history, the qualities he looked for in used guitars and fuzz boxes, were those with the force of being to cut a wound in the numb skin of pop.

A month before he died, Quine gave me a CD of Lester Young's last sessions. Young, nearly dead from alcoholism, could hardly get the notes out, while the muscular rhythm section behind him didn't cut him an inch of slack. The disconnect was almost total: and still, Lester won, he cut them all—his soul bleeding through that cold machine. Moments Quine lived for, while he could.

The Attack on Artists' Rights . . . and Me

Long before Google, it was common for publishing companies to play a game with composers to whom royalties were owed: they would simply not mail out their royalty checks unless the composer complained. They figured that if they withheld 200 composers' checks, twenty would never complain—and, years later, they could quietly pocket the money. Publishers weren't usually brazen enough to try this with major composers or rich stars—the type of people likely to have their own accountants on retainer. But for middle-level composers/authors, it was a common scam.

One such composer was Frantz Casseus, who had put out several records on Folkways, and had a tune covered by Harry Belafonte—but he wasn't rich, not by a long shot. He managed to get by, taking in students like me, building his own guitars, making his own furniture, and decorating his tiny apartment through what he called "mungo hunting"— finding cool stuff at flea markets or on the street.

In the mid-'80s, Frantz suffered a series of strokes that left him unable to play guitar. His marginal financial situation quickly became desperate. A friend of Frantz's who had volunteered to help organize his finances discovered that income was being withheld, and confronted the publishing company. They responded predictably: "Oh, we just didn't know where to send the checks." (Frantz had lived at the same address and with the same published phone number for over forty years.)

Several months later a check arrived for $16,000. By this time, Frantz was living in a nursing home and had been forced onto Medicaid—so everything went straight from his bank account to the government. Still, it wasn't the financial loss that bothered Frantz most. I'll never forget what he said as he stood there, finally holding the delayed check in his one good hand: "If I had known, I would have composed more. I felt my work to be without value."

Frantz died less than a year later, without ever returning to composition, leaving behind a body of work beloved by Haitians and classical guitar fans to this day. I still play his pieces sometimes—and have many happy memories—but I remain haunted by those words, and the questions they raise about his life, and ours.

There's a ghost in the room when government roundtables of distinguished "stakeholders" discuss the size of the incentives our Founding Fathers provided when creating copyright protections. Big Tech's bean counters can supply mountains of data on the dangers (to them) of providing too great an incentive. But who will speak for the work left uncreated if we set the incentives too low? How can an accountant measure the loss of a work's absence? Who can place a value on the ineffable, immeasurable might-have-been? These days, as the tech industry attack on artists' rights threatens to make Frantz's loss into the new normal,

I think of him often, of what might have been, and what might never be.

If we judge the work Frantz might have composed by the work he did, then the loss—to Frantz, of the dignity of work; to us, of the beauty his work might have created—is profound. I try to weigh the profundity of that loss against the banality of the publishing company's decision to not pay him—the entirely logical corporate decision to use the existing legal landscape to maximize profits. The company risked no liability for withholding the checks, and stood much to gain. The math is simple, and those doing it rarely see their victims.

And although the publishing scam described above remains common, it was never the norm. Other forms of theft occur even less frequently: for example, using copyrighted material in films or television commercials without a proper license is relatively rare. Why? The answer is certainly not because film/commercial producers are more morally correct than publishers or record company execs. Instead, it's because composers/artists have the legal tools to sue violators' pants off.

Ultimately, Frantz's human tragedy and our cultural loss come down to the lack—or presence—of certain legal tools. Bean counters will always count beans; the ethics of the system reside in the structure that predetermines the math: a structure of laws that limit the liability of corporations for not locating a composer/author; or place the burden of notification on the author; or limit our access to information; and so on. Little details, arcane language, in print so small you wouldn't notice.

* * *

In the end, Frantz got his check: and for all its abuse by corrupt institutions and individuals, the system functioned in some way: most working composers, artists, and musicians would eventually get paid. Many were cheated, but there was a common understanding that not paying the composer or artist was in fact cheating.

This is no longer true. Google's corporate lobbyists are aggressively trying to create a new legal landscape in which their drive to profit without paying creators will be unobstructed, our tools to win fairness obliterated. They want to put virtually all uses of our work in the same legally vulnerable position that enabled Frantz's publishers to rip him and so many others off.

And they've become rich and powerful enough to get away with it.

Sometimes the changes are dramatic, like the creation of "safe harbors" enabling advertising brokers like Google to reap huge secondary profits from brokering ads amid black market theft of our work. Often they're not: an "orphan works" proposal designed to make nonpayment just profitable enough, to make artist recourse just expensive enough to be beyond the reach of most, to make accountability just murky enough.

And this is why I've spent years writing letters to Congress about orphan works, parsing the boundaries of fair use, and helping to get other artists to do the same, when I should be practicing guitar: because when we produce something that people would like to hear, I want my work, and Frantz's work, and the work of all other cultural creators, to be valued. And when our work is producing profit, I want its creators to have their fair share.

* * *

It all comes down to value: will we as a society choose to value cultural creativity, or not? When Frantz felt deprived of value those years when the checks didn't arrive, it wasn't because he was in it for the money. Frantz gave up his chance to live a comfortable life to become an artist, because he was doing what he loved.

But for better *and* for worse, money is how value is measured in our society, it's how we know others care about what we do, and yes, it's how we survive. And until the day when that ceases to be true for all of society, musicians, recording artists, writers, photographers, filmmakers, graphic artists—we who create so-called content, we who do the work of art—are going to demand economic justice. We're organizing to fight back, and we're going to win. We may not have the deep lobbying pockets of the tech corporate giants, but we can do something they can't: we can speak the truth, and the truth is a powerful slingshot.

Maybe There's Something There: Three Short Riffs on Derek Bailey

1. From an e-mail to a friend, 1/1/06

Did you ever hear Derek play live? When playing with really loud noise, rock, funk, or punk improvisers, he still did this amazingly delicate and detailed stuff, as if he were playing solo in a quiet concert hall, often completely inaudible unless someone happened to listen back to a multi-track tape (at which point they would be astounded: check out his work with the Ruins or with Jamaaladeen Tacuma and Calvin Weston). As if Derek wasn't going to let the fact that he was painting a mural by the side of a speeding superhighway prevent him from drawing miniatures. Stopping the car, walking off the road, seeing the details yourself—maybe it was all part of the intent.

2. "Free Improvisation"

Describing the subjective experience of playing music before a live audience (or the imagined future audience of a recording session), writer/cellist Richard Sennett ("Resistance," *Granta* 76, 2002) claims he's "yet to meet the musician who walks on stage with the same insouciance he or she might feel . . . practicing in private . . . [There is] no return to the Garden where we play unselfconsciously . . ."

Sennett obviously never met Derek Bailey. If Derek hadn't reentered the Garden of immanence, he certainly sounded as if he had, somehow making a separate peace with the Obstructing Angels. In fact, Derek sort of lived in the Garden, spending his musical life in that moment most terrifying to most musicians: the completely unscripted.

Why is this moment so terrifying? I don't know. But in memories of my own first attempts to improvise freely after having been "trained" in classical guitar, rock, blues, and jazz, and in my experience of working with musicians new to the concept, I know there's an instinctual terror of this moment, usually evidenced by an inability to start, or, once started, to stop.

In free improvisation, beginnings and endings juxtapose "the piece," whatever it is, with a silence more ontologically complete than that of other performance. The absence of sound at the end of the jazz, classical, or rock piece is filled with the comforting presence of the next piece—on music paper, in memory, in the rules of a shared tradition.

And I suspect this is linked to the nervousness I've felt among inexperienced improvisers. The palpable fear of beginning from, of returning to . . . silence/nothing . . . is an expression of the fear that the sounds you make won't compare favorably with the silence which preceded/follows it. This in turn represents a deeper fear. In music, too, silence may equal death. The suspicion that both are preferable, and all this implies, is among the oldest of terrors.

Friedrich Nietzsche, in *The Birth of Tragedy*, referred

to the ancient Greek awareness of this "wisdom of Silenus" as the unacceptable shock which stung the art of classical theater into being. That's what the devotees of free improvisation get for their troubles: to occasionally witness the birth of tragedy, the moment when fear sucks beauty into the world, live, onstage, before their very ears.

I don't think Bailey or other experienced free improvisers experienced conscious terror in performance. The most notable aspect of Derek's performance was the calm pleasure, and often amusement, he seemed to take at diving into nearly any musical situation. But, in addition to the personal courage it takes any artist to begin a new form, to persist for decades in a music most people find difficult and are only too happy to ignore, it should be said that Derek Bailey, in the process of music making he pioneered, was a man of deep ontological courage.

3. Adapted from the liner notes to Derek Bailey's recording, Ballads *(Tzadik, 2002)*
When Derek Bailey, the most here/now of musicians, decides after so many decades to record jazz standards, it means something special. I've always felt, and I think Derek would agree, that the past is usually past for a reason . . .

And so, what has Derek Bailey been up to? I phoned and asked him.

"It was Zorn's idea."

"The fact that I was going to play a standard did something interesting to the improvising."

"I bought this guitar that was totally inappropriate for playing standards, but . . ."

"I'm not interested in Improvised Music with a capital M. I'm interested in improvising."

"I thought, *Maybe there's something there.*"

The resulting recording is unlike anything I've ever heard. The playing throughout is stunning. But what's most striking is Bailey's method of relating the received text of the standards to improvisation. Of course, even in free improvisation, what emerges from imagination is largely what went into memory, or some synthesis of its elements. In addition to the standards being covered and a whole lot of the jazz history around them, I would guess the Improvisations of Django Reinhardt and the Theme and Variations pieces of Webern also went into the hopper. Normally distant cousins, these emerge from Bailey's composting as a single voice.

Bailey made *Ballads* by interweaving long stretches of improvising and jazz standards in a single continuous performance. The standards are beautiful. The improvising parameters draw on the vocabulary of free improv and are far wider than those normally employed in jazz. Yet I don't hear this as a pastiche work, juxtaposing a preconceived concept of "free improvising" against a preconceived idea of how to play "jazz standards." The approach is integrative, with standards informing the improvising and vice versa. How they do so is both mysterious and strong.

Even for people who do a lot of improvising, it's difficult to improvise freely once the idea of a structure has been introduced. It's practically a reflex, at least among those musicians with enough training to actually play a jazz tune, to cling to the raft of the nearest song structure, even if it's sinking (and, in these situations, it usually is).

Derek Bailey's mastery is evident in his ability to resist this temptation and let the song be what it is while letting the improvisation go where it goes. The beautiful paradox is that this doesn't sever the relation of song to improvisation, but creates deeper, less predictable relations.

World Music: Time and Money

TIME

1. Emile Yoan

From 1980 through 1982, I played guitar in a group with the displaced Ivorian griot Emile Yoan. The group's practice—what we did at rehearsals—was to find parts in relation to Emile's already composed electric kalimba and vocal parts (Emile told us these compositions were communicated to him in dreams by his dead brother). Our accompanying parts were arrived at through long trance-inducing improvisations.

It became my job to transcribe tapes of the improvisations so musicians could remember their parts at the next rehearsal. It soon became apparent something was wrong. The accompaniments which had meshed so perfectly with the kalimba at previous rehearsals would, in spite of my painstaking transcription, sound completely wrong when repeated.

At first I thought I must not be paying enough attention to detail in the transcription process. Then I thought Emile must be confusing the song titles, exchanging the kalimba part of, say, "Poem" with that of "I Love You Mama." Emile insisted this wasn't the case. Finally, by comparing kalimba-part transcriptions of the same tune from different rehearsals, I figured out what was going on.

Emile's kalimba and vocal parts were, in fact, completely consistent from rehearsal to rehearsal, and corresponded with the same song title every time. What had confused his American accompanists was his nonlinearity. Emile's kalimba parts were based on repeated two-bar figures. But for him, the identity of the figure wasn't determined by which eighth note it started on. He could start the figure at whatever point in its sequence he felt like. The phrase was identified by what it was, not where it started or ended.

For Emile, time was round.

2. Alfredo Pedernera

From 1987 through 1989, I worked as guitarist for Evan Lurie's nuevo tango band, with the great Argentinian bandoneonist Alfredo Pedernera. Alfredo's English was somewhat limited, and I used my almost equally limited Spanish to help communicate Evan's instructions during rehearsal.

It was obvious from the first rehearsal that I was in the presence of a lyrical genius on the level of Lester Young. Alfredo's improvisations were astounding. Technical mastery and tango dramatic flair were fully evident without ever obscuring the emotional depth of his playing. His vocabulary was enormous, drawing freely from tango, Western "classics" (he knew "The Revolutionary" by heart), and, I'm sure, a whole world of Argentinian pops songs I would never have recognized.

The one limitation of Alfredo's playing seemed to be rhythmic. Getting him to sight read the rhythmic component of Evan's charts and play them in time with the rest of the ensemble took extensive repetition. At first I attributed this to the nature of tango musicianship. White Argentinians killed or exiled almost all of their enslaved Black population early in the country's history (after having switched from an agricultural to a meat-based economy), and suffered the loss of African musical influence. What remained is still the most European of all South American musics. Spanish and Italian influences—free cadenzas, frequent tempo changes, extensive use of rubato or pulse—are particularly strong. Local Indian tradition, for all its charm, couldn't bring back the funk.

Still, tango came into being as a twentieth century dance-related form (first popular among the subculture of gay sailors). And when I went to hear Alfredo play in various Argentinian restaurants with his own trio (contra bass, classical guitar, bandoneon), his time was excellent. The band rocked.

I began to notice that even in Evan's rehearsals, Alfredo's difficulties varied depending on what the other musicians, in particular the guitar and bass, were playing. The closer we were to one of the normal figures of tango, the easier Alfredo found it to read and play in time with us. This was true no matter how fast the tempo or how complex the chart.

Incredibly, what tripped Alfredo up the most was when the bass would play simple quarter notes, the most elementary rhythm for North Americans, what we're taught to silently count underneath other rhythms even when we don't play it. We had learned every rhythm we knew against that simple beat. Alfredo hadn't.

It's our peculiarity to have attempted to measure nature by placing it on a grid of equally divided parts. In our pride we've come to mistake these grids for nature, to believe time itself is shaped like the uniform metronome or stopwatch clicks by which we measure it. Alfredo knows differently. For him, our steady numbers dance around a preexisting shape. The world is measured against a map of tango.

3. Susana Baca Ensemble

At the 2002 Persona festival in Köln, Germany, one of its organizers told me why he preferred polyphonic music: as a metaphor for the ability of the mind to contain multiple ideas simultaneously. For this reason, he said, he preferred contemporary classical music to jazz. Wonder what he would have thought about the "Black Peruvian" music of Susana Baca.

I'm not sure whether the idea of having me and various other downtown NYC types overdub on Susana Baca's record *Eco de Sombras* originated with producer Craig Street or someone at Luaka Bop. It almost certainly didn't come from David Pinto, the bass player/arranger and, with Susana, composer of much of the band's material. David, as I came to discover, is a highly sophisticated musician with a working knowledge of North American jazz and rock, plus idioms from Brazil, Cuba, Haiti, Peru, Mexico, European art song, and classical music. If he'd felt the need for postmodern genre juxtapositions, atonal/polytonal or noise elements, he would have written them into the arrangements. On first listen, the basic tracks seemed to me extraordinarily beautiful and complete. I doubted I could add anything useful. I told this to Craig, who assured me that they were looking for only a few added textures to subtly broaden the sonic palette and do nothing to mess with the integrity of the band's sound.

From the beginning, it was clear I was missing some basic information on how the bars were being subdivided. The eighth-note pulse was clear enough, but, lacking a chart, I sensed I was grouping the eighth notes differently than I should have. In trying to write out what I was hearing, I kept coming up with isolated odd-metered bars. I knew from my limited study of other Latin American music this was almost certainly not how the music was conceived, a sure sign I was feeling it backward.

A few months later, I met the band. The occasion was the record release party at Joe's Pub in NYC. When I saw the sheet music, I realized that in at least one of the pieces ("El Mayoral") I had been completely mishearing where "one" was, hearing the bar offset by a quarter note. This wasn't accidental—the aural signs which allow the listener to distinguish one from three, upbeat from downbeat, are culturally determined. My signs were not only missing, but in many cases reversed.

The bass, drum, and guitar lines were doing everything possible to imply 3/4, and the players were in fact hearing three superimposed over four. For example, in the cajón parts, the second eighth note of the second triplet is accented, thus placing the first accent after four eighth notes. The uninitiated would naturally tend to hear this as the downbeat of a third quarter note.

Now, it's okay to rock the boat: the music is supposed to

be challenging, and a lot of Black music engages the audience by continually frustrating rhythmic expectations. The more the musician implies alternate time signatures, alternate ways of rhythmically framing the material, the more the listeners increase their engagement, fighting to keep the beat against the calculated challenges of the musicians.

Pulling this off requires a complex shared musical language on the part of musicians and listeners. The musicians can challenge the listener (and each other as listeners) precisely because they know both their own and the audiences' limits. With a clear common language, musicians can rock the boat.

But in my case, the boat had tipped over into a different understanding of where "one" was. Does it matter if there is no common understanding of "one"? After all, most of the US audience, sharing my own cultural background and limitations, misheard right along with me.

If you believe art has something to do with communication, it does. Rhythmic structure is part of the syntax of music, a prerequisite to the creation of meaning. Conflicting understandings of where one is don't constitute a dialogue— there's no language without syntax. Imagine someone moving both hands one inch to the left on a typewriter keyboard and typing as if they were in normal position.

Although sounds can be heard without being rhythmically framed, it's doubtful that meaning can be created (unless, of course, it is the "meaning" of chaos); the rhythmic place of the note or phrase determines whether it functions to create tension or release. Culturally, rhythmic placement determines whether a note or phrase is heard as weird or normal, other or self.

While musical effects will of course occur, they won't be related to the intentions of the artist if that artist doesn't know where one is. My musical role seemed to have inverted: the "downtown" improvisers with whom I'd done most of my collaboration over the last twenty-five years mask a reality of shared language (we know where one is, even if the audience doesn't, and if there isn't a one, we share the rules of the alternate games of pulse or polyrhythm) beneath a spectacle of disjunction and chaos (noise). Here, I was attempting to mask a reality of deep disjunction beneath an uplifting world music spectacle of shared language. One is mimesis—maybe of some kind of social disjunction. The other is a form of lying. I found myself wondering what was really being bought and sold, and why.

It also matters to me personally for a different reason. I find in those rare moments of mutual hearing among musicians a lonely instance of the suspension of narcissism (German pedagogues please note: "instance of," not "metaphor for").

I found my ignorance embarrassing, and promised to go home and practice—not playing, which I could do passably enough, but hearing. By the time I realized the Peruvians were subdividing into four groups of three, I'd become used to subdividing the 12/8 bars into three groups of four.

To have learned or heard correctly in the beginning would have been difficult; to relearn was more so, even though what I had actually learned was a composite which "explained" my mishearing by shifting between different ways of counting and imagined, occasional odd-metered bars to fill in the gaps. To learn the music correctly wasn't simply a case of intellectually understanding the shift in counting and adjusting my foot tapping accordingly; each bass line, each guitar part and vocal melody, had to be painstakingly reheard, reimagined, relearned.

A dramatic shift in meaning accompanied the change in counting: what had, in three groups of four eighth notes, been a light folky groove with a mild syncopation became a virtuoso exercise in rhythmic tension. Counting differently changed the song "Panalivio," for example. In three groups of four, it's a Grateful Dead lope; in four groups of three, a tightly wound spring of funk tension. In three, a Christmas song; in four, the song of enslaved Africans forbidden to play their music outside of a Christian context.

The tension between these two ways of counting/hearing is culturally weighted: the triplet feel of the four groups of triplets signifies West African music. The eighth-note feel of the three groups of four eighth notes signifies Europe. The actual musical histories are much more complex—both histories contain both ways of hearing, and both use the device of superimposition of three against four, four against three, etc. But Black Peruvian music was developed by people forced to hold two ideas in consciousness at the same time, a forbidden past, an unsupportable present; forced to hide resistance beneath a performance of complicity.

The lyrics of "El Mayoral," the song I had found the most difficult to hear correctly, describe the hidden preparation for a violent uprising against enslavement. The harmonic progression—root, fifth, sixth, seventh—is so common it's used in North American baseball games (you know, the thing they play when nothing's happening that starts slow and gets faster and faster). That this comforting march has been rhythmically offset by an eighth note makes it something else entirely, the ability to read this subtle détournement a matter of life and death. Does this matter? To my ears, yes.

Many years, one CD, and a number of gigs later, I still find the music difficult. But I'm beginning to understand. These musicians have developed an ability not simply to alternate between the different possibilities, but to actually place the musical content within different time frames simultaneously, to count in multiple systems. If notes derive meaning from their placement within the rhythm, then we can understand what these musicians are doing: generating multiple hearings, extracting multiple meanings from the same melodic object.

If a literary analogue must be found, it isn't metaphor, which, in gesturing past its original meaning, impoverishes it. It's closer to metonymy, in which a word, phrase, or even a single letter may generate multiple meanings (Talmudic rabbis rocked the house at this) without displacing the original text.

This is part of what Susana Baca's musicians—and to whatever extent the music is funky, all musicians in African-derived forms—are "playing": the generation, by rhythmic means, of a polyphony of meaning.

AND MONEY

This story should end here, on the word "meaning," in the semiotics of the eighth note, at a comfortable level of abstraction, and with the optimistic implication that difference can be, if not surmounted, at least approached, given time, effort, and a will to know. But there's something else.

The musicians in Susana Baca's band continue to work and tour the "world music" circuit: some with Susana, or with other mostly South American artists. Still, when rates of pay for the recordings, gigs, and short tour I did with Susana Baca were being determined, the gap between the Peruvian regular members of her ensemble and the NYC "special guests" was probably roughly equivalent to the difference between the military budgets of our respective countries.

Does this matter? Earlier I wrote: "Does it matter if there is no common understanding of 'one'?"

If you believe art has something to do with communication, it does.

I was hired for Susana Baca's band in spite of my lack of musical qualification in order to present an uplifting spectacle of social solidarity—of communication and "oneness"—across cultural/national/racial lines. Behind the props, there was a reality of musical, linguistic, and economic division. This doesn't mean we were fighting: Susana and her band were great to tour with—Susana is a poet whose intelligence and warmth would make itself felt across any linguistic divide; she and her band were genuinely nice and funny people; and if there's such a thing as a shared humanity, we shared it (and maybe a bit of weed, wine, etc.), and we shared some musical values as well.

But we also knew I couldn't find the downbeat. And the differences in pay aren't just a hangover from the history of racism and colonialism whose injustices Susana's lyrics describe with such elegant passion, but a continuation of that history.

* * *

Alfredo Pedernera moved to Miami, a geo-compromise between his wife's desire to remain in New York City and his own wish to return to Buenos Aires. Many of the CDs and film scores to which Alfredo contributed a large dose of tango credibility have received wide distribution, and some of the composers for whom he played in New York have gone on to considerable success. Alfredo himself played mostly in Miami restaurants. He died several years ago, and his own immaculately notated set of compositions remains unrecorded.

Emile now lives in housing located for him by the Department of Human Services. He was never able to become a full-time musician.

Emile has always been a highly resourceful man—or, to put it another way, a brilliant hustler—making his way alone and broke from Senegal, through France, to the US. He worked as a bouncer at a bordello in Paris, played kalimba in the subways of NYC.

I don't know what he did for money during the two years we rehearsed together on and off—our infrequent gigs didn't produce much of it. But Emile always had some kind of hustle going on which paid the bills, and he never managed to let it interfere with his optimistic energy.

The boundlessness of this optimism was a source of some friction between us. For example, he once described the audition for Amateur Night at the Apollo as "a gig for $50" without mentioning that we only actually got the money if we passed the audition, returned the next night to play the show, and came in first out of dozens of acts.

During most of the 1990s, Emile's main day job was at

a security guard agency. In 2001, he had a stroke and was unable to continue this job. He was placed on disability, which meant that in exchange for his medical benefits and around $600 a month, he was no longer allowed to work.

He became despondent over this, the continuing effects of his stroke (which hurt his ability to sing and play the kalimba), and his extreme poverty and isolation. Emile had always put off visiting the Ivory Coast until after he'd landed a record deal which would both pay for the trip and allow him to return in triumph. During this time, his parents and several of his sisters had died, and he'd lost touch with the rest of his family. But Emile managed to borrow and save (he worked off the books handing out leaflets for stores) just enough for a one-way ticket. His plan was to use his bank card to access his Social Security payments, which were deposited into his New York bank account.

He gave me his conga drum before he left, and promised to write. But Emile had picked a bad moment to return: an increasingly bloody civil war threatened to turn the Ivory Coast, peaceful and prosperous for almost half a century, into another Rwanda. When I didn't hear from him after almost a year, I imagined the worst: that he'd had another stroke or been killed in the fighting.

What actually happened was even stranger: if there were any surviving members of his family, Emile was unable to locate them. The situation around him became increasingly violent. But when Emile's cash ran out and he tried to access his bank account, he was told there was a problem that could be resolved only by his being physically present at the bank's NYC office.

How Emile, still partly disabled from stroke, managed

to survive the next eight months without money or connections in a war zone is a mystery to me, but testimony to his skill as a charmer. All I know is that when the US embassy finally flew him back to NYC, he left behind a young fiancée and a promise to bring her to the US before their baby was due.

Although he's still in possession of the multitrack Afropop tapes he's been working on for years (mostly with an engineer/producer who donated studio time), he hasn't been able to land a record deal. Lacking the finances for pressing a CD, self-marketing, website development and maintenance, and so on, the indie route hasn't been a realistic option for Emile.

We saw each other occasionally for a while, and I helped when I could. But sometimes he hustled a little too hard. I gave him back his conga drum, which I think he sold. But I wouldn't sign the papers guaranteeing his fiancée wouldn't become a ward of the state.

Emile eventually brought his young son here: super cute, super smart. Christian drew wonderful things with crayons at my kitchen table. He died at the age of eight, supposedly of pneumonia. I went to the service at the evangelical church in Harlem to which Emile had become a fanatical convert. Its leader, "Mama," chose the occasion to remind nonbelievers of our destination in the lake of fire. Later, Emile couldn't understand why I was so stubborn. We lost touch.

The children of "It's a Small World" dance in a circle whose empty center is a lacuna. The term "world music" erases the prefixes that would have defined a relationship ("first" and "third"), thus enabling a dialogue between center and periphery that reifies the power relationships it refuses to name.

Indeed, it is a small world after all. One that's getting smaller all the time.

Still Things That Move: The Poetry of Henry Grimes

For most of his career, the poet Henry Grimes (1935–2020) worked as a jazz bassist. He was one of the top-call musicians of the 1950s, recording/performing with Gerry Mulligan, Sonny Rollins, Thelonious Monk, Anita O'Day, Benny Goodman, and many others. But he's best known today for his association with the free-jazz movement of the '60s. In addition to gigs with Cecil Taylor, Pharoah Sanders, and Archie Shepp, Henry played on the seminal ESP recordings of Albert Ayler's group and was central in creating this historically important sound and process. In this format, Henry recorded some of the most powerful and original bass playing of the twentieth century.

Two years before Ayler's murder, and increasingly uneasy in New York, Henry moved first to San Francisco and then to Los Angeles, where he lost touch with the music community. He lived in SRO hotels in a notoriously bad section of downtown LA, often working as a day laborer, without access to a bass. Neither addiction nor alcoholism contributed to this situation; Henry just fell through the cracks and disappeared.

However, during this time Henry filled hundreds of notebooks with handwritten poems, as well as stories and essays.

> *. . . But the forceps of a dawning year*
> *to draw the time*
> *with measures oblique of filling,*
> *to the satisfying of the soul,*
>
> *So, to God—that we may all fill—our bowls,*
> *Until we are delivered . . .*
> —from "The Ground"

The conditions under which Henry lived can only be imagined; he rarely speaks of them now. But the above poem/prayer for a full bowl (and "deliverance" from the world) reflects an experience in which hunger is more than just a metaphor. Jarring to realize that Henry's hard times occurred so near the center of the Hollywood film/music industry, less than five miles as the crow flies.

But that crow almost never flies.

Henry remained in exile from music for over thirty years. He probably would have remained so indefinitely had he not been tracked down by Marshall Marrotte, a social worker and jazz fan with access to Social Security records.

On learning that Henry was back on the scene, I immediately contacted him and began to plan a project, which eventually became the Spiritual Unity quartet and CD. We've worked together on and off for some years now, and my admiration for his bass playing has, if anything, grown.

Nevertheless, I was at first skeptical when asked to read Henry's poems. In my experience, skepticism about amateur poetry is usually justified. And, in Henry's case, I had to wonder how a man who almost never speaks could write.

Then I read the poems.

What I find beautiful in Grimes's poetry is not the social history of its creation, practically an archetypical version of the poet as romantic victim. The work stands on its own, without this. But why should it have to? Does anyone ever read Paul Celan without thinking of the personal history out of which he wrote, the injury to language that his words were being asked to redeem? Henry's need to bend language, to play with, to reinvent, to break syntax, emerged, like Celan's, from both historical and personal circumstances that broke the language of the past.

In an essay entitled "That Silence Thing," the composer/pianist Anthony Coleman writes: "Being a musician . . . arises out of all kinds of loves, desires, and drives. But . . . it also arises out of a basic mistrust of the descriptive and/or emotive power of verbal language." Henry's first choice of music as a language can be read as a rejection of written or spoken language; when this option was no longer available, poetry had to become possible.

For Henry Grimes, as for Paul Celan, "Language remains unlost, in spite of everything."

> *Yes, do pages of phrases*
> *Write*
> *motion, still things—that*
> *move, that have lines in mystery . . .*
> —from "Monk's Music"

IN MEMORIAM

I met Henry Grimes in sound long before I met him in person, through the recordings of Albert Ayler. And it was only after several years of listening to those recordings that Henry's work began to emerge for me from among all the other remarkable musicians on those recordings. In fact, it was while listening to a copy of *Swing Low Sweet Spiritual* given to me by Robert Quine that we both realized we were hearing something special—the way Henry managed to walk a line between soloist and supporting role on that intensely beautiful recording still amazes me. And before I even met Henry, I would play this record to other bassists, saying, "Listen, listen . . . hear what's possible to do on your instrument."

So it was like a miracle to me when I got an e-mail from Margaret Grimes saying that he was alive and well, and looking for gigs in NYC.

That first gig began an education that, for me, was to continue for the next seventeen years. I learned that Henry never played what was expected, rarely played the chart, and always played something much better as a result. In the following years, we made two recordings (*Spiritual Unity*, with Henry, myself, drummer Chad Taylor, and the late Roy Campbell Jr. on trumpet; and *Live at the Village Vanguard*, with Chad, Henry, and myself) and did many gigs and tours, during which I got to know him as a friend.

Henry was the very opposite of the technocratic "chops monster" that haunts the bad dreams of conservatory students. He was a someone for whom life had burned away the inessential, leaving . . . a soul. His wife Margaret shepherded Henry's beautiful and extraordinarily gentle soul through a world of increasing brutality with great love and dedication, for as long as was possible.

Although Henry was a man of few words, his presence transformed any space—train compartment, stage, recording studio, or even, finally, a nursing home dormitory. That quiet power was the spirit of the instrument Henry loved—transforming the music from below, building the structures from which others swing. The contra bass language was the speech of his heart.

Together, in the trio with Chad and the quartet with Roy, we played the most beautiful music I've ever experienced. I'll miss Henry, and will always feel lucky to have had the chance to hang out with him and make music while we could.

Songs of Resistance

Originally written in 2017 as liner notes to
Songs of Resistance 1942–2018, *Marc Ribot
and various artists, ANTI- records*

My grandparents lost brothers, sisters, cousins, aunts, and uncles in the Holocaust, and I've toured and have friends in Russia and Turkey: we recognize the likes of Donald Trump, and it's no mystery where we will wind up if we don't push back against the ideology that created him.

It's not that things before Trump were any picnic: the many victims of racism, sexism, homophobia, xenophobia, and war under earlier presidents—some of them Democrats—cannot be forgotten; and even among the politicians for whom I voted, few were willing to address the structural causes of these problems. But even the most pissed-off of my activist friends knew right away that Trumpism was seriously wrong, and that resistance—not just protest, which by definition acknowledges the legitimacy of the power to which it appeals—had to be planned.

I'm a musician, so I began my practice of resistance with music. Normally, I practice by studying the past ("Ancient to the Future," as the Art Ensemble of Chicago put it—and as Hannah Arendt might have if she'd been a jazz musician), and then blowing on or reconstructing or simply misreading those changes until they become useful in the present. So, to prepare for this moment, I went back to archives of political music and listened again—trying to find what was useful now. I uncovered songs from the World War II anti-Fascist Italian partisans ("Bella Ciao," "Fischia il Vento"), the US civil rights movement ("We'll Never Turn Back," "We Are Soldiers in the Army"), a political song originally recorded by Mexican artist Paquita la del Barrio, disguised as a romantic ballad ("Rata de Dos Patas").

I also wrote songs: things I heard at demonstrations, and newspaper and television stories that I couldn't process any other way, wound up as lyrics. I changed these found texts as little as possible: much of "Srinivas" is a metered version of news articles on Srinivas Kuchibhotla—an Indian immigrant murdered in February 2017 by a racist who mistook him for a Muslim. And John Brown of the eponymous song really did kill five slaveholders at the Pottawatomie Creek.

I make no claims of historical "authenticity" about the arrangements of archival songs on *Songs of Resistance*—although I hope they work on more than one level, the arrangements and composition songs on this album were written and performed, without apology, as agitprop. I borrowed from, referenced, and quoted public domain songs as much as I could, wanting to harness the power of our rich traditions to the needs of the current struggle wherever possible. For the same reason, I altered texts and arrangements freely, as political songmakers have always done.

The underlying politics of this recording is that of the Popular Front: the idea that those of us with democratic values need to put aside our differences long enough to defeat those who threaten them. Although this approach has its frustrations, it worked last time around (1942–45).

Coordinating a multiartist recording like this wasn't easy: although the musicians involved were without exception enthusiastic and helpful. But the madness of the moment kept us moving when things got bogged down: we recorded Justin Vivian Bond's "We'll Never Turn Back" literally while Donald Trump was delivering a friendly speech to antigay hate groups in Washington, DC. Tom Waits's "Bella Ciao" was recorded near Santa Rosa, California, in the haze of smoke from 1,500 homes destroyed by wildfires attributed partly to global warming. Not a day goes by that I don't think about the fact that we're living through what may be the last years of possibility to lessen the degree of catastrophic climate change which will be experienced by our kids.

And what I think is that thinking isn't enough. The same can be said of singing.

Profits from this album were donated to the Indivisible Project, a 501(c)(4) organization with chapters in every congressional district, which works to build the local and national networks we need. I have a lot of friends who think that any kind of politics isn't cool. I appreciate the sentiment, but we need to get over it, roll up our sleeves, and get our hands dirty if we're going to survive this thing.

Although my intention in organizing the recording was to express solidarity with everyone victimized by the Trump regime, finding a way to express that solidarity without repeating old patterns of oppression is not easy. I hope the dialogue and spirit of solidarity begun among the performers on this recording will continue with its listeners and spread even further.

Postscript

The question of "the good fight"—how to fight an enemy without becoming it—hangs over "political" art (as the question of truthfulness hangs over art claiming to have transcended the political). Indeed, Left and Fascist song do share musical commonalities. (Armies fighting for causes good and bad all need songs to march to.)

The recordings on *Songs of Resistance* won't resolve that question. But I've noted a difference between the marching songs of fascism and those of the partisan and civil rights movements: a willingness to acknowledge sadness:

"We are soldiers in the army . . . We have to fight, we also have to cry."

"And if I die a partisan, goodbye beautiful, goodbye beautiful, goodbye beautiful. Please bury me on that mountain, in the shadow of a flower."

"I am a pilgrim of sorrow, walking through this world alone. I have no hope for tomorrow, but I'm starting to make it my home."

"A thousand mill lofts gray are touched by all the beauty a sudden sun exposes. Yes, it is bread we fight for, but we also fight for roses."

These songs' acknowledgment of human frailty, of the fact that "we have to cry" even as "we have to fight," is for me a sign of enormous strength. Their vision of a beauty beyond victory is also a sign of hope, a reminder that we at least have something worth fighting for.

Playing Hal Willner Home

1. Love and Acoustics
In the studio, most producers sit in the control room, where the expensive speakers allow them to hear what's being recorded with the highest fidelity. Hal did that sometimes.

But other times, he liked to sit with the musicians—in the middle of the rhythm section, or the string section, or near the bell of a saxophone during a wild solo, with his headphones on like the rest of us, his head down and his eyes closed, "feeling the music." What ineffable spirit was Hal chasing there—beyond EQ, balance, and the thousand parameters of the "control room"? Was it some god or essence? Some spiritual core? I don't know. But I know that Hal loved music like few others, and that what he heard in it was something he deeply needed, something transcendent, something miraculous. And I know that we, the musicians, loved Hal.

2. Time
Bill Frisell wrote: *I'm very sad about Hal. Can't imagine this world without him in it.*

I replied: *It's like waking up and finding the Empire State Building gone. But I guess we in NYC should know by now that this too is possible. We can't take one minute of time with the people we love for granted.*

So many called or wrote when they heard the news in April 2020. People spoke and cried at Zoom gatherings; some of us played. But it hurt, almost physically, to be so "close" to other musicians who knew Hal, and not be able to play together—Albert Ayler's "Bells," or "Didn't He Ramble" . . . or the theme song from *The Three Stooges*. Whatever. That's our tradition: when a musician dies, we play our brother or sister home.

Big "Time" mattered to Hal too. Not so much "history," as memory. Hal and I shared ghosts—Hitler was always in the mix, muted, but still pinging the VU meter; Lenny Bruce and Allen Ginsberg too, and the others who tried to make "poetry possible after" . . . by laughing, fucking, loving, getting high—*living*—as much, if not as long, as they could.

I'm writing code now, but you can read me, can't you, Mr. Jones? Cause that's what "we" do: write code, read it, become it . . . It's what "our" world is made of, and reading is our life: downtown no-wavers, postpunks, loft jazz geniuses, and occasional lost-in-the-[rock]-stars reading Disney, Monk, Mingus, Weill, etc. Hal's genius was to make those readings happen.

3. Hustling

Of course, Hal was a hustler too. He had to be, in order to make his crazy projects work. He knew how to harmonize bios as well as notes, and he had a finely calibrated sense of the exact ratio of rock star to avant-whatever needed to make the powers that be cough up a budget.

Sometimes this got Hal into arguments with his downtown friends—possibly even me, once or twice. But in the end my sympathies were with Hal. Maybe because I'm a bit of a hustler myself. But what really ends all debate is this: Hal Willner got a show in which Al fuckin' Green and Syd Straw danced in a fuckin' mambo line to the Sun Ra Arkestra playing "Space Is the Place" on national fuckin' network TV. And you didn't . . . right?

4. Family

Sometimes Hal seemed like a comrade in some crypto-commie sect so secret that even its own cadres didn't know it existed. Or maybe we were fellow worshippers in a heretical branch of Judaism whose weird set of sacraments and (Black musical) saints masked our orthodoxy. But yeah, although inclusive of people from all over the geographical and social map (and a few beyond it), Hal's mysterious project had something to do with the Jew thing.

I remember Hal in his bad old days, in an apartment on the east side of Tompkins Square Park, literally on "Charlie Parker Place," where he slept surrounded by literal stacks of Lenny Bruce live tapes, before the place burned down. Hal really dug Lenny Bruce, and, through his work, created a tunnel between Bruce's world—its TV shows, jazz, obsessions, Yiddishisms—and our own, locking old Beats and hippies into studios together with young postpunks, jazzers, and aesthetic radicals who hadn't yet figured out who their LES parents were. What the Cairo Geniza library was for ancient history, Hal was for the history of pop and jazz culture from the 1940s through the 1970s: his archives and memory held details of the past that no one else had (and few would probably even want).

But all together, those details mapped a language. Lenny Bruce's parents spoke Yiddish. So did Hal's . . . so did mine (at least, when they didn't want me to understand). But they were the last generation who cursed in Yiddish when they stubbed their toe (or, at least, who cursed in Yiddish on the tenor sax). I curse mostly in English, and, beyond a few Yiddish phrases and some broken Italian, speak it. But even if I learned Yiddish, it would signify "Jew," not "NYC."

Lenny Bruce's language signified New York—a particular Black, Latino, Jewish New York in which Yiddish was taken for granted as part of the mix: "If you live in New York or any other big city, you are Jewish . . . even if you're Catholic . . . If you live in Butte, Montana, you're going to be goyish even if you're Jewish." Clearly, Bruce's "Jewish" was also particular: not generic, not sanctioned, inclusive of all NYC, producing hallelujahs from sex, drugs, and postbop.

Maybe Willner can be accused of loving Lenny Bruce's world to the point of nostalgia—forgetting its sexism, casual homophobia (even among some of its gay writers), racial codes, and other not-so-sweet etceteras. But I think Hal's real love was for its language—and his deep project was to preserve and translate. Will people be able to comprehend a Lenny Bruce monologue in fifty years? What will our music mean when they can't? It's hard not to feel, with Hal's passing, a piece of our own language going with him.

Part II

EVERYBODY'S A WINNER

We Tell Children the Cow Says Moo

When my daughter was small, I taught her that the cow says "moo," the sheep says "baa," the rooster "cock-a-doodle-do." But rarely do we really listen to animals, and even less often crawl (or ask our children to crawl) into the abyss of what they mean.

Some years later, in a suburb of a small town on the island of Culebra, Puerto Rico, I listened. The roosters in Barriada Clark begin not "at the crack of dawn" (must we always clothe the naked in cliché?) but much earlier, at around three or three thirty a.m. I often find myself awake around this time—my sleep habitually broken—and so became a more or less captive audience for the roosters' performance.

As it turns out, roosters don't say "cock-a-doodle-do" either; instead they emit a strange scream, punctuated into roughly three sections, mounting in pitch and intensity from strangled indifference through frustrated protest to a final glissando of abandoned rage. This sharp cri de coeur emerges from silence, without prelude, and dissolves back into silence without coda or diminuendo. After a pause of about ninety seconds, the same routine begins again.

More often than not, I lie awake with what my late guitar teacher Frantz used to call "the night terrors"—fears and regrets presenting themselves, at least till dawn, as "lucidity." The sound world of the animals disturbs my sleep, and perturbs my involuntary wakefulness. I'm sure the animal behaviorists can explain very well the function of the rooster's cry—but what accounts for its disturbed aesthetic? What makes it sound like a cry torn from the rooster's soul, like some drunken Zampanò, screaming hoarsely back at the bouncer who ejected him and the thousand who rejected him before, opening a crack in a mirrored hallway stretching all the way back to childhood, the original wound reopened with the latest bloody lip?

The rooster's unmistakable rage (like Zampanò's) seems directed as much at the destiny which traps him in his sex as at the human world which breeds or slaughters him. Whatever function of mating or marking of territory their cry performs, they seem to take as little pleasure in their alleged male dominance as the brutalized vet in Springsteen's anthem (so famously misread by Ronald Reagan) did in being "Born in the USA."

The final insult of the rooster's performance is its repetition—its identical expression, again and again, without variation, development, or history. What perturbs is not the sound itself but its paradox—the mechanical repetition of passion. Shouldn't something so passionate be spontaneous, not memorized or—worse—involuntary? And shouldn't the spontaneous change with mood or circumstance? The effect is like hearing a jazz trumpet player one had believed to be improvising "freely as a bird" repeat the same solo note for note, night after night; or of overhearing the object of one's desire whisper familiar intimacies to a stranger.

It's not difficult to understand the motivation of the fake trumpeter or the prostitute. But who pays the roosters? Not just one, but a whole orchestra, screaming their thwarted purpose into the night, again and again, locked into brute antiphony with the animals in other yards, other barrios; punctuated only by a cow's low despair, a sheep's desperation, and, toward dawn, the fucking of cats, fighting of dogs, or occasional pan-barnyard riot.

Trapped in their repetitive world of blunt expression without language, with no hope of understanding, their cries seem to beg not human butchers, but their own animal god, to slaughter them, to strangle them, anything to release them from this silent, howling life.

A Portrait of the Poet
as a Young Asshole

Second grade started out predictably enough, another stone-faced middle-aged lady teaching us whatever the fuck they told her to. But then Miss K. died or was outed as a child molester or something. How the hell could I know? They never told us shit. Anyway, one day she didn't come back. After an enjoyable week of torturing substitutes, my classmates and I were restored to order by one Mrs. Gladknee.

Yup, that really was her name, though I was never sure about the spelling, an uncertainty related to the fact that Mrs. Gladknee never taught us spelling . . . or math, or cavemen and dinosaurs, or where bauxite was produced, or any of the other knowledge Miss K. had tried to impart. Instead, Mrs. Gladknee tried to uplift our tender spirits through The Arts: which meant we spent all day drawing with crayons and singing.

This sounds like more fun than it was . . . Mrs. Gladknee was, as her name implied, resolutely Glad, fairly bursting with strange enthusiasms. But her resolute cheerfulness inspired resistance in those of us—me, the emotionally unstable Stanley D. (later to pull the tail off a rabid squirrel he had cornered in the boy's room), and Margery C. (future leader of a Trotskyite sect)—who were already skeptical of such militant optimism.

We got tired of drawing flowers and horses and stick-figure boys and girls. Pressing leaves between wax paper and making stencils of snowflakes also eventually lost their respective charms.

But we actively hated "singing": which meant endless repetition of happy songs that Mrs. Gladknee had learned wherever she was from. It seemed like the songs were always pitched right for the girls but forced the boys into a high key, revealing the fragility of our newly acquired masculine identities. We resisted by pretending to be even worse singers than we were, ironizing the melodies like a chorus of soprano Richard Hells.

I remember only one fragment of a lyric: "Up on the rooftop, one, two, three . . ." something to do with Santa and his merry whatever. This was pretty bad. But even worse was the accent: Mrs. Gladknee's "roof" didn't rhyme with "proof." Phonetically, it was closer to a dog's "ruff." I didn't know where such accents originated, but wherever it was, I didn't want to go there; each "ruff" filled me with passionate loathing.

One sunny day, Mrs. Gladknee decided to expose us to "poetry."

After a brief demonstration of what "rhyme" meant, we were set free to each create a poem.

Even in second grade, I knew there was more to poetry than just rhyming. Any asshole could rhyme—even "up on the ruff-top, one, two, three" rhymed with some damn thing.

A poem had to open to the ineffable. Even I knew that. And so I began with the best metaphor for ineffability I could think of:

"Who has seen the wind?" I scribbled. *"Neither you nor I . . ."* I was on a roll.

When, naturally, I finished early, I stole a look at Nancy G., seated in the desk to my right. If I'd only known then what I know now, I would have said I had the hots for Nancy. But in my polymorphous ignorance, all I felt was an overwhelming urge to fight her: physically, preferably in the wrestling format, down into the schoolyard dirt. (Although not necessarily, mind you, to win.) Reasonably enough, I interpreted this to mean I hated her, and I was always getting in trouble for creating casus belli. Like I said, they never told us shit.

Anyway, Nancy was supposed to be the smartest kid in second grade, and what was she writing? Some bullshit about her dog, who loved to "roam." To my left was the budding beatnik Peter D., hard at work expressing his innermost sadness at the rain. Rhyming "roam" with "home"? Using "rain" as a metaphor? Jesus fuckin' Christ, gimme a break! I was gonna kick everyone's ass on this one. I smirked as I confidently handed in my paper.

And yet even before Mrs. Gladknee finished reading our poems, I could feel trouble brewing. She was uncharacteristically grim for a while, then approached my desk, slowly, ominously. "Marc, this is a very nice poem. But . . . is it *your* poem? Did you make it up yourself?" She squinted down at me through rectangular reading glasses from the heights above her well-corseted tits, and I squinted back, trying to play it cool.

Part of me was genuinely confused by her question: it hadn't actually occurred to me how a poem I related to so deeply couldn't be mine. Of course it was mine. Who the hell else did she think wrote it on the five light-blue lines of my yellow school paper, Charles Olson perhaps? And my poem was fuckin' good—better, I was certain, than the roam/home/sad rain crap my classmates were giving her. So what right did that woman have to question my integrity?

On the other hand, I had absorbed enough Western culture to sense that, somehow, I had transgressed. And I wanted to avoid the consequences. "Yeah, of course it's mine," I sneered, gambling on the margin: of all the millions of books in the whole world, what were the odds that Mrs. Gladknee had the same edition of *Children's Garden of Verse* that I did?

Unfortunately, the odds turned out to be better than I'd hoped.

I was hauled in front of the class and made to sit like a mini Eichmann in his Jerusalem glass cage, while Mrs. Gladknee used me as Exhibit A in explaining the Serious Crime of Plagiarism to my classmates.

This was 1963. "Postmodernism" had yet to be invented; "Pierre Menard, Author of the Quixote" had not yet been written; the mathematics that would later enable YouTube were still in the theoretical stage; most of the pseudointellectual defenders of its attacks on copyright hadn't entered pre-K; and Richard Prince was just gleam in his (or someone else's?) father's eye.

So my options for a defense were limited, and I sat there with head bowed in mute embarrassment while Mrs. Gladknee raged on—comparing me to Hitler, Stalin, and Elvis Presley—and Nancy G. gloated.

But inwardly I swore—like Scarlett O'Hara in *Gone with the Wind*, or like the hero of any Hollywood action movie—that someday, somehow, I'd get my revenge.

I never did, of course, although I did later punch Robbie M., who had laughed and given me the finger in my moment of shame. But the defeat of my Hollywood revenge fantasy seemed in keeping with what was to become a trope for my generation. As the actual Richard Hell sang: "You gotta lose, you gotta lose," you can't win all the time. While defeat isn't synonymous with ineffability, early experience of the winds of adversity can certainly teach you to bow down your head.

At the end of the teaching year, Mrs. Gladknee was forced to resign after someone upstairs discovered she'd faked her teaching credentials. No one in my class was surprised. And it turned out that wasting a precious year of our education with a total fraud didn't matter. Most of us eventually learned spelling anyway. Nobody ever gave a shit if we knew what bauxite was, or who produced it. Some of us lived, some of us died. Some became rich, others poor. Some found love, others never did. Stanley was eventually locked in a nuthouse. Nancy died of cervical cancer after a so-so career as a jazz singer. Robbie M. made a fortune in commercial real estate. Looking back across half a century, I can't see clear lines of causality in any of it . . . life seemed determined, if not predetermined, by some indefinable force beyond our knowledge. We could never see it or grasp it, only bear helpless witness to its effects.

I Watched from My Room as the Bicyclist Was Run Down

I watched from my window as the bicyclist was run down. It happened in front of the train station in Nijmegen.

The auto was making a right turn, the bicyclist was going straight.

They collided.

I was on the fourth floor of the Hotel Mercure, in room 402.

My window was open.

I heard people shout, saw a crowd gather.

An ambulance came and took the bicyclist away, unmoving, perhaps dead.

Policemen interrogated the driver.

The crowd dissolved.

I closed my window and ordered room service.

Carrot ginger soup, garnished with parsley.

Everybody's a Winner

So he says to the former love of his life: "Sure, I'll meet you downstairs."

She was returning something borrowed . . . a weird musical instrument used as a prop on one of her fashion jobs. He knew she hated art-directing fashion shoots. She was in fact an excellent painter, a truth confirmed for him by the fact that she had a street-level Chelsea gallery, and by his own reaction to her painting, which, like all art he loved, always cracked him up.

But "a gig is a gig," as they both liked to say—and she actually did say that after showing him iPhone evidence of an adolescent supermodel's professionally made-up lips grazing the mouthpiece of his antique French horn.

"Meet you downstairs" was code meaning he didn't want to sleep with her. It was an unnecessary message, because she didn't want to sleep with him either, and wouldn't have even if they'd met upstairs. She was in fact happy with her girlfriend. And she hadn't slept with him at all since their breakup years earlier (except that one time: an experience that at first brought elation, then confusion and rage—the very emotions whose shattering but predictable repetition had caused the breakup).

Of course, the real address on the coded "downstairs" message was his own. But it was a letter he never bothered to open, since doing so would have meant reading his wish to "protect" her from the imaginary pain of his imaginary rejection of her imaginary desire as projection, masking a certain contradiction, a great big suitcase of confusion he wasn't prepared to unpack.

He didn't want to go there, wherever "there" was, especially since he had just proposed to his girlfriend, who happened to be out of town, and who happened to be slightly jealous, and who, in fact, he happened to love.

Of course, the former love of his life deciphered all this—and his many other codes—with ease, and forgave his half-conscious hypocrisy, because meeting upstairs would have triggered associations of her own, and she didn't want to go there either.

And so, between their inability to go "there," and the inability of either of them to imagine really going anywhere else, they had found this:

They were friends.

Several decades earlier—during one of the many ons in their on-again, off-again relationship, before "on again, off again" had become a routine, and routine became intolerable, and intolerable became dangerous—they had imagined the people they would in time become . . . and laughed.

Walking drunk on sake and desire down East 2nd Street, at the magic moment when the growing light of dawn hadn't yet overpowered the exhausted streetlamps, and the last stray club kid staggered oblivious past the first ambitious Wall Street–bound early bird, they had literally stumbled onto a work of "visionary" art. Someone, no doubt one of the many gifted lunatics who frequented the LES at the time, had stenciled the words *Friends My Ass* in bold white letters on every square of pavement the entire length of the block. Their immediate and mutual recognition of the visionary's truth had cracked them both up.

"We'll never be friends," they had whispered, making out against the metal fence of the old 2nd Street graveyard, before stumbling home to make each other cum. Maybe they hadn't whispered low enough, or perhaps their lust had disturbed the sleeping dead . . . but something tempted time, and time had taken its revenge.

As another downtown crank had once written: *"Go to him, he calls you / You can't refuse / When you ain't got nothing / you got nothing to lose."*

And so they met downstairs, returned the French horn to his basement locker, and went out for Thai. He told her a joke about a moth and a podiatrist. She laughed, and told him how weird fashion models are. They talked about their respective kids, and mutual friends, and the Rammellzee retrospective at the new Red Bull gallery, which had really cracked him up.

It was June, and sunny, and they sat in the back garden of the Thai place on Court Street. For some reason, the loud air conditioners that seem to be required in all outdoor NYC eating spaces weren't blasting that day. They drank iced coffee and it was lovely.

Parting had its own bittersweet semiotics. "Does Janet still hate me?" he asked.

"No," she said. "She knows I'm meeting you, and it's okay. But yeah, she still feels a little weird."

He had wanted to tell her about proposing marriage to his girlfriend, but instead just said, "Cool, see you next time."

He wondered if, when he finally did tell her, she would be sad, or fly into a rage, or be happy for him . . . Or maybe they would drift politely apart and never speak again. His awareness that these fears too were projection provided no comfort.

On his way back upstairs, he tried to imagine whether there would ever be a time when he, the former love of his life, her girlfriend, and his girlfriend would all sit down together in peace.

He imagined Janet being cold, competitive, defensive, like the last time.

He had tried so hard to be nice, agreeing with everything she said, but she refused, pulling the cape of her agreement away at the last minute like a matador, leaving him stumbling and awkward.

He imagined himself saying: "Look, Janet, you don't have to be angry anymore. It's okay. You won. You got the girl. And I won too. See? We're all sitting together with people we love on a beautiful late-spring day, drinking iced coffee in this lovely Thai garden. See? Nobody lost. We all won. Everybody's a winner."

That's what he imagined himself saying.

Pale Blue Eyes

Jews are a bitch, no? My great uncle Jack married (or did he ever actually marry?) a woman named Dot, who wasn't Jewish. When they met, he was a cab driver who probably also did illegal liquor drop-offs, etc., during Prohibition. She was an "actress," probably actually a chorus girl. But they never had kids. It seems they were waiting for Jack's mother to die first. At least that was the reason Jack gave. They waited and waited, and by the time she finally did die, Dot was too old. At some point, they moved up to Monticello, where Jack slowly worked his way up from playing the horses to having something to do with managing the track.

They had a little house on a country road, the first people I knew who lived in "the country," and Aunt Dot was always very patient and loving with us kids, in a quiet, understated way. She took me on walks and taught me how to pick blueberries and blackberries. She gave me milk to drink straight from some farmer's moo-cow that tasted miraculously good compared to the stuff we got in New Jersey. Uncle Jack was a skinny guy with glasses who cracked a lot of jokes. He carried me on his shoulders while we made the rounds of bars with names like "Thoroughbred Lounge" and "Tip Sheet," showing me off to his racetrack buddies.

Years later, after Dot had some kind of operation, they moved to Florida to be with Jack's spinster sisters, Gert and Blanche. We had never seen much of Gert and Blanche when we were growing up on account of some ancient dispute between them and their sister-in-law, my grandmother. The dispute had something to do with them "kicking her when she was down," i.e., when she was facing painful decisions about whether her husband, my never-met grandfather, should end his beautiful but drug-addicted life in a mental institution or a TB sanatorium.

Before Florida, Gert and Blanche had lived in New York. The one time we did visit their apartment on Central Park West, I remember how stale and dark it was. It seemed to have no windows, and I was amazed people could get used to living that way. *Maybe this is how people like it in New York*, I thought. They were nice enough, smiles for the kids and everything. Gert, quiet and servile; Blanche, the former career girl, outspoken and intellectual. According to family legend, she had been married once to a perfectly nice man but had left after a few months to move back in with her sister. No one ever figured out why.

There was something else that bothered me about Gert and Blanche's apartment. Being a kid, I of course couldn't name it. But I think had I been an adult I would have said it stank of incest. Maybe not the tongues and fingers and unmentionable penetrations type of incest. Maybe. But I felt the fierce gravity of some black hole of the familiar, some emotional dark star from whose compacted mass no light escapes. I remember emerging from the cramped elevator to gasp in the sunshine and fresh air on Central Park West.

Anyway, they gave my parents boxes and boxes of books to fill up the empty shelves of our new house in South Orange.

I never saw Dot during the Florida years. Every now and then, photos of the latest visit to the relatives would get passed around, including a picture of a Dot I no longer recognized, fat instead of tall and dignified, sunglasses hiding her pale blue eyes. There were reports she was losing her sight, rumors she wasn't getting along so well with the sisters. I guess they must have been true because one night she left their house and drowned herself in a canal.

Uncle Jack just pushes on and on into his nineties, past operations, birthdays, in and out of tragedies. He sleeps during the day and stays awake at night, much to the consternation of the sisters. His raspy gambler's voice on the long-distance line to New Jersey says: "Seymour, I can't stand it anymore. They're driving me nuts." Old people say the darnedest things.

Aunt Blanche says: "Seymour, what can I do? He won't take his medicine, he won't eat. The doctor says . . ."

Jack makes passes at the housekeeper. He gives the doctor firm instructions: no heroic measures. Do not resuscitate. "Look, Sy," Jack wheezes, "nobody lives forever . . ." And it's hard to tell, over the phone, whether he's coughing, laughing, or both.

It Was Almost Like Paris

Woke up early this Sunday morning. Early (groan) considering the hour and condition of our going to sleep. Direct sunlight was shining through the top part of the side window—consuming a chair, some shoelaces, a sleeping dog—just like it does for three months of every year, beginning in late April, ending in September, strangely vanishing for a month around the summer equinox, and for all of the dark winter.

What had woken me? The telephone sat undisturbed in the dust on top of the TV. The unset clock blinked on and off. Pascale lay next to me, face buried in the pillow. It was so quiet, I could hear her breathing. I could hear a train go by underground.

That was it—the machines were off! It was the Sunday before Labor Day, and when the evening shift left, the factory across 16th Street had shut down the machines, maybe till Monday night.

Pascale smiled. She was awake. "Listen, I never noticed that before . . ." Beyond the cars on Eighth Avenue, you could faintly make out the ringing of church bells. In seven years in the five-story walk-up, neither had I.

"I like that," she said. "It's almost like Paris."

O Say Can You See

American life is lonely.

I call you sometimes, when I'm off the road.

We have coffee near your stop on the N train.

The trains are slower now.

Most often, I don't call.

In our fantasies, we're the *Honeymooners*, or *Seinfeld*, or the cast of *Cheers* or some other sitcom—always wandering into each other's private spaces unannounced.

"America Mourns *M*A*S*H*," the headlines read. "Psychotherapists on Call for End of TV Dynasty."

Even Alan Alda cried a little.

We found more time when the kids were little to go to the park, or the bowling alley.

Now we're busy. I'm writing a million e-mails while supposedly working on my solo album. You're . . . what is it that you do when you're alone?

In *M*A*S*H*, everyone knew what everyone did. Thin tent walls and public mess halls left every human foible exposed to Alda's venomous sneer.

It was funny.

They were there to fight the Communists.

Communists had the nerve to choose such living situations "voluntarily."

Communism equals war minus death. No dignity. No privacy.

"They were like a family to me," said the weeping woman in the *Daily News*.

In Rome, the film score recording sessions began at ten a.m., and ended promptly at seven. A huge Rube Goldberg device attached to the projector carried the celluloid film through whatever pathways the length of the looped scene demanded, at precisely twenty-four frames a second.

The studio was grand, paneled in some kind of blond wood, big enough to accommodate an orchestra. Sometimes, channels at the edge of the board crackled with neglect, but it was no problem: there were other channels.

Sometimes Benigni stopped by to see how we were doing.

At one p.m., we did as the Romans and broke two hours for a three-course lunch: antipasto, primo, secondi, dolce, café.

This was not what we were used to in the NYC bunkers where indie musicians score indie films by the lamp of the midnight oil amid the detritus of takeout Styrofoam and cold coffee.

"Indie means independent," I explained to the worldly Italian producer.

"Yes, I know," he responded, lighting a cigarette. "I've worked in America before. It reminded me of being in the military . . . a huge army organized for production."

It was a memorable meal, but that's all I remember.

It happened a long time ago, during the "Italian miracle."

Before Berlusconi.

Before the euro, the crash of the euro, and the inevitable restructuring, whose austerity will no doubt become what passes for fate.

When you've driven to the edge of America, as far north as you can go, past Augusta, past Bangor, past Houlton, past the fenced-off SAC base at Limestone and the last all-night Dunkin' Donuts, up where "the wind blows heavy on the borderline" and the long winter's wear and tear has made your Kodachrome superfluous months ago, then you're at the end of America, the border, the limit.

But for Canadians, it's just the beginning.

And here's what every Canadian—in fact, everyone in the world who's not American—knows about America: it is the land of sex.

And that's why you're here, in a hotel bar in Van Buren, Maine, in 1976, standing in a matching wide-collared outfit with the rest of your band, scratching out the chords to "The Hustle" on a cherry-red '67 Melody Maker while off to the side, on a stage consisting of a dirty rug and plywood thrown over packing crates, the "exotic dancer" contorts and grovels listlessly while five or six drunk potato farmers aim Canadian nickels at her pussy.

They mostly miss, but she's too medicated to care, her "dance" always threatening to devolve into crawling, twitching, or sleep.

Somehow, implausibly, it's afternoon . . . and what gray winter light manages to pass the filthy windows enters an uneasy alliance with the red of the single stage light's cracked gel, an unhealthy blend not flattering to the human form. Every now and then a gust of cold wind and bright light from the exit door strips the last "exotic" defense from the naked dancer's now only too familiar flesh.

In front of you, your lead singer Kay goes slightly cross-eyed trying to puff out a breathy melody on her flute in time to mouth the song's only lyric:

"Do the hustle."

A year later Kay would get all banged up trying to make a gig in Fort Kent (last stop on Route 1, which begins in Key West) during a blizzard. But today, she and her leaky flute are in fine form.

Maybe Kay's equally sturdy French Canadian girlfriend Donna had come with the band on this run, and was sitting in the back drinking heavily and scowling at the potato men. (Donna's ancestors had drifted across the border with the lumber trade. There was a derogatory name the Maine Yankees used for these other Acadians, but you've happily forgotten it.) Maybe Donna hadn't come after all.

Strippers who couldn't make it in NYC went to Boston. Those who couldn't make it in Boston went to Portland. Those who couldn't make it in Portland went to Bangor. Beyond that was the "exotic dancer" circuit . . . a stripper's equivalent of the glue factory. A similar map could be drawn for professional musicians.

The band would play five sets a day on weekends—two in the afternoon, three at night. During the breaks, everybody climbed the dusty stairs to their narrow rooms above the bar, you to lie in your bed staring at the ceiling, the "dancer" to make some extra bread turning tricks with the potato men.

We were all doing the hustle.

* * *

"People see porn and puritanism as contradictory, but they're just the flip sides of the same American coin: sex without affection, affection without sex."

"Thas pretty good, Ray," I slur, already a bit drunk from the Irish whiskey at Charles's informal wake. Charles wasn't Irish, but Ray, our mutual pot dealer, was . . . and on occasions of state—all too frequent in the mid-'80s—the whiskey came out, and Ray transubstantiated into the grungy LES version of the working-class priest the Cleveland Jesuits had tried—and might well have succeeded, had he been a little less gay, or a lot more hypocritical—to convince him to become.

Charles had died of the plague, of course. The wonder was that he held on as long as he did, having not only been a rent boy in the NYC epicenter of the worst years ever for the oldest profession, but having specialized in work that others refused: scat calls in particular.

Does that mean he allowed other men to shit on him, and/or shit on other men? I wondered at the time, but respectfully refrained from asking. (It was, after all, a wake.)

But yes, it did.

"It was always the Midwesterners, the Protestant choir boy types, who went the craziest when they hit the city," Ray eulogized, remembering Charles's farm-boy good looks and bright-eyed, if somewhat twisted, enthusiasm.

That conversation took place in a rent-stabilized building on Second Avenue and East 4th Street. Now the building is no longer rent-stabilized, and the apartment is gone, and most of the people in the room that day are gone.

A few of us are still here, though, doing whatever it is

we do; traveling, like the nontourist natives of Venice, "in the seams of the city"; recognizing one another on the street by secret signs, the invisible stigmata of memory.

The Lido of Something, Near Ravenna

I walked on the beach today, the Lido of something or other, near Ravenna. Even now, I can't walk on the beach without remembering the thrill it gave me to find shells. They were my first objects of desire, my first wealth, my first treasure. And unlike the money I would try to collect later, they were beautiful in themselves.

Even now, some of the thrill remains when I find them at the water's edge, still beautiful, free, and there for the taking.

But I no longer dream of shells at night. And I no longer collect them.

Now it's ghosts and broken memories of shells I collect in my light-blue bucket, and lay out, still glistening wet, on the table, in the vain hope you'll share my enthusiasm, asking, "See? . . . See what I found? . . . See what I brought you?"

Kaddish for Joan

Joan was the child of a Jewish/Christian marriage—her mother, Rebecca (née Liebman), an actual Marine during the Second World War, crazy and cruel to her children as her own Jewish-Polish peasant-in-Brooklyn mother had been to her, as their world had been to them all. Her father, Richard Petersen, a reasonably lovable drunk, provided whatever shelter there was from Rebecca's rages, violent and unpredictable even before her institutionalization.

Richard's parents were cute old Swedish American immigrants, pancakes for breakfast and spartan-but-not-too-weird values, probably a better bet as role models than the frightened old couple in the dark apartment on Brighton Beach Avenue, where the quiet dreaminess of faded photos under glass couldn't disguise something guilty and strange, a vacant sadness no American child born in the '50s could fathom.

Growing up on the goyish side of town of Palo Alto with long straight almost-blond hair and Nordic looks, Joan must have found it easier to identify with the Petersen side. But had you asked her at the time, she would have found the idea of identifying with anyone, especially anyone old, ridiculous: she was going to be herself. (People used to think things like that in America.)

To the sixteen-year-old Joan, this meant being an artist and a rebel: having boyfriends who sent her clay models of themselves in tiny clay caskets with little poems about suicide on the back, making clothing for a pet rat in home economics class, and nurturing a bitter sense of the absurdity of the adult world.

The look of exaggerated innocence with which she faced/excluded that limiting world had fooled almost no one since she'd been nine, and was the opposite of the look of mischievous complicity with which she won all her younger cousins as permanent allies in the generation wars. When her mother had a breakdown, slashing the California night air with a steak knife, Joan came to stay with Marty's family for a year. Marty's mother was Rebecca's sister. Marty was thirteen and Joan was seventeen. She was the first artist he'd ever met. She was his hero and he was in love with her, hopelessly and completely.

At twenty, Joan was a hippie living in the East Village, studying painting at Parsons, and living with a pipe-smoking skinny boyfriend named Charles. Marty was taking LSD and playing guitar in a high school rock band. Although it's easy in hindsight to draw a connection between the enthusiasm with which they embraced their counter-cultural outsiderness and certain aspects of Jewish history, nobody in our 1970 world would have done so, and had an adult tried, they would have found it further proof of the general stupidity of adults. Marty and Joan were hippies. That was all the identity they needed.

It wasn't till much later that things changed, and then only slowly, in a peculiar way.

Joan began to know hardship early in life. At twenty-two she was pregnant and abandoned by her boyfriend, now insane. Stories filtered down of him driving west in a stolen car, hallucinating himself as Ulysses S. Grant. Marty didn't see her often in those days—he had moved north and had disasters of his own. The adults who had been the objects of her silent ridicule in former years were in no rush to help now that she was desperate. On the contrary, they took satisfaction in the defeat of the proud hippie. Let it be a lesson. There was talk of a suicide attempt. In her hour of depressed, pregnant, homeless need, the Brighton Beach grandparents had let her stay in their spare room, but only for a few days, and with strict conditions: she was to understand that they were decent people, mindful of the opinions of their decent neighbors, and their primary concern was that she do nothing further to shame them.

Joan disappeared, moving somewhere near Baltimore. Peace wasn't made until the baby was almost six. What she experienced, none of her relatives would ever know, but when Marty saw her again at a family seder, she was properly chastised by life and poverty. The old look of complicity was gone, edited out along with anything else that might interfere with her new project of ingratiation with the "adults." *You'll come around*, the new look said to his skepticism, with a plastic smile whose very rigidity was the last reminder of her former self, like a tiny dissenting footnote lost behind the author's desk: it referenced *The Stepford Wives.*

Painting was also gone. After a time of panic and hard unemployment, Joan had taken an administrative job in the Glen Burnie school system.

It was then that Joan first began to be Jewish, to use

occasional Yiddish phrases, inflections, or gestures she'd learned from the grandparents or comedians on TV. "What can you do?" she'd ask with that accent, not wanting an answer. Then she'd shrug and raise her eyebrows just like the Brighton Beach grandma. She began to resemble the grandma in form as well, a process of weight gain seeming to parallel her spiritual transformation.

It worked. The adults (Marty had come to realize that his family would never apply this distinction to downwardly mobile members such as himself) slowly came to believe in her repentance. Her rehabilitation was considered complete when she married Ed, a boring but successful accountant ten years her senior. "You gotta have a sense of humor," Joan said, while Ed impressed Marty with stories from the '60s, when he was, you know, "Heh heh heh, kinda radical." Joan looked apologetic. "So you adapt . . ." she said in The Voice.

Joan was really in it now. She'd drive up from Maryland on Passover to give the kids a taste of Jewish culture. The plaintive shrug of the grandmother who had once treated her with contempt now draped her shoulders like an old shawl. "That's life," Joan said, to the benign approval of the adults. How nice to see her finally coming home, back to her culture, back to her people, her family, her roots. Finally accepting herself. "Family is so important," she said.

It didn't matter what was said in The Jewish Voice, or that it was clearly put on, or that Yiddish gestures were never used to express anything but clichéd defeat and resignation. As long as she used them regularly, she was part of the club. Another triumph for Jewish self-acceptance.

The last time Marty played Baltimore he connected

with Joan and the family for dinner. Ed repeated his '60s stories once again, while the kids looked out the window or listened to death metal CDs through headphones. When Ed finally got up to piss, Joan leaned over, locking Marty instantly into their old conspiracy, her eyes glowing with manic excitement for the first time in decades. "Marty, it really happened, it's not a joke. They beamed me up onto their spaceship, and they talked to me. It happened to one of the neighbors too, so I know I'm not crazy. They're from a very ancient civilization and they came all this way to show us how to live in peace . . ." And love, and all the other things the old Joan used to believe in.

Sometime later, in a synagogue somewhere on this too-familiar Earth, Marty found himself standing for the words, "Mourners, please rise."

"*Yitgadal v'yisgadav, shamai rabba . . .*"

Ten or so stood there, mumbling the half-familiar kaddish along with him. Marty scanned the English translation in vain for a reference to mourning. Another one gone into death, another into madness lost, solid gone, gone away for good . . . and all these holy fools could think to do was give expression, week after week, to this fanatical need to praise.

Clearly someone had made a horrible mistake.

The Twenty-Three-Day Tour

Once there was a musician who went on tour. He flew to Frankfurt, took a train to Krefeld, and played. The next day, he awoke at 8:35 a.m. to take a train to Schondorf, and he played there. The following day, he woke at 7:20 a.m., took several trains to Tübingen, and he played there. Normally, the local promoters would give him money to take a taxi to the station in the morning, but sometimes he forgot to ask them and would have to pay himself. That morning in Tübingen was just such a time. Nevertheless, at 6:37 a.m. he was on the first of several trains to Vienna. The concert was well attended.

The next day, he took the train to Mestre, an industrial suburb of Venice. He played, ate in an Italian restaurant, and the next morning took the 7:49 to Ljubljana, one of his favorite cities.

The following day was listed in his itinerary as a "travel day," which meant that he had no concert that night. Instead, he took the 4:35 train to Lyon and slept in a compartment which had been reserved for him. In the middle of the night, he woke up and watched the lights of houses go by.

He arrived at 9:30 a.m., and played the concert at 9:30 p.m. The concert was part of a festival of jazz music, a type of engagement at which his agent continued to book him even though he often questioned whether it was really appropriate.

The following day he played in Fribourg. The day after that he played in Geneva. The day after that he played in Bregenz. Several years earlier, he had wound up making love with a woman who had attended one of his concerts in this town. As it turned out, she still lived nearby. After the concert, they were able to have a reunion.

The next day at 8:17 a.m. he took the train to Schwaz, a very small town. The day after was another "travel day." He took a bus to Munich and an airplane to Lisbon. At the hotel in Lisbon, he was able to do his dry cleaning. The following day, he went by airplane to Ghent. His ticket to Ghent was a round-trip ticket, which the travel agent had said was cheaper than purchasing a one-way. He had been exposed to this type of apparent illogic on the part of the airlines before, but it always troubled him.

After playing in Ghent, he went by train to Lille, a city in France. The concert hall there had a peculiar acoustical quality which he enjoyed. The following day, he took the 10:43 to Rotterdam. The ride took six hours and thirteen minutes. The day after that he played in Amsterdam. At 7:23 the following evening, he took an all-night train to Dresden. Again he looked out the window at the passing lights.

When the musician arrived in Dresden, it was 9:33 a.m. He checked into the hotel and, since it was a city he had never visited before, decided to go for a walk. His hotel was in the Neustadt section, on Nieritzstrasse, and he walked past the reconstructed Dreikönigs church, past a bas-relief of Rosa Luxemburg, onto a kind of Euro-mall where the cute new post-Communist shops all seemed proud and somehow pathetic.

He stopped into the local record store long enough to determine that they had never heard of his record, and then proceeded onward toward the Augustusbrückce, trying not to inhale the famous East European morning mix of coal fumes and Trabby exhaust.

As he drew nearer the skyline of the old city, he began to make out the statues. They seemed to be everywhere: pouring fountain water out of vases, playing lyres, sitting on top of triumphant horses, mourning dead kings, whispering ideas into the ears of poets, driving chariots drawn by tigers.

Conditions were especially crowded along the tops of the old buildings, where the statues seemed to conduct a life of their own; larger, older, and undoubtedly better than the lives of the people who walked in the street.

The trumpet-blowing angel on top of the bombed-out Kunstakademie reminded the musician of the two chariots above the city of Rome, one set atop a theater by some late emperor, the other, facing it from across the city, installed under Mussolini. He thought of certain friends of his who had very long historical memories, and wondered whether this was always a good thing.

A few hundred yards from this fortunate angel lay the black ruins of the Frauenkirche. Actually, the musician loved ruins. "Maybe it's because I was born in Newark," he mused, and was annoyed at the construction cranes which were busily at work restoring and erasing the past.

The musician walked for a while without thinking, till he found himself in the landscape of empty plazas and gargantuan Communist buildings which surround the old city like a moat. A sign informed him that one of these buildings was the Deutsches Hygiene Gymnasium. The shininess of the buildings and the peculiar deadness of the spaces between them jogged repressed memories of traumas in the suburban shopping malls where he had had his own identity forced on him. Their oversize scale made him feel as though he were walking in place, and so he stopped.

It was extremely quiet. The coal smells of the morning had almost dissipated. A few meters away stood an untitled statue of a Stakhanovite woman worker. The musician stood admiring the statue's gray impassive face, eyes focused on the distant future, strong arm raising a hammer. He noticed that someone had placed a sprig of fresh azaleas at her feet.

The next day, the musician was tired. He had drunk more than usual after the concert and had what the French call a "*gueule de bois*"—face of wood. He did succeed, however, in catching the 11:19 to Berlin.

He arrived at his hotel at 2:17 p.m. still feeling tired. There were several urgent faxes from the booking agent waiting at the front desk. He should have answered them, but instead went up to his room, hung his suit bag in a closet, and sat in a chair doing nothing for a very long time.

Putting Your Arms around a Memory

In 1992, I signed the lease to an apartment on Second Avenue, between 5th and 6th Streets. My prior residence had been a cheap hotel in the East 20s where I'd moved when the woman I'd been living with on East 6th Street and Avenue A kicked me out. I shared the hotel room with an ancient electric fan and a rust-stained sink (into which I guiltily pissed when too messed up to make it to the bathroom in the hallway). Walls and ceiling were covered by a graffiti mural illustrating a particular NYC take on the Hindu cycle of death and rebirth, an enormous Krishna plucking up the souls of the dying, hurling them out again as babies toward a Lower East Side–looking slum.

After pondering the transitory nature of existence from this privileged position for several weeks, I gained the strength to go out apartment hunting. I got up early, bought black coffee, and picked up a *Village Voice*. Unsure if my strength would last, I took the first apartment I was shown and lived there for the next fourteen years, excepting the four it took for another attempt at cohabitation to go sour, during which time I used it almost every day as my office/studio.

The apartment was small, consisting of a hallway from which branched, on alternating sides, a kitchen, bathroom, and bedroom. Each of these had a window on its respective airshaft, but the back bedroom window opened onto a block-long inner courtyard

The previous tenant, Ilwan Dilage, had left his nameplate on the doorway, a Formica table and single chair in the kitchen, and a metal single bed frame in the bedroom. Ilwan, like the landlord whose secretary rented me the apartment, like many of those who actually maintain the shaky rides of that "Coney Island of the mind," had probably been Ukranian, and—I don't remember now whether I heard this from the building's old superintendent, or just made it up—had died in the apartment, spending his last weeks in the bed I inherited. This didn't bother me, or any of the various companions I shared it with once I started "dating" again. In fact, I thought Ilwan's ghost brought good luck, and used his death-metal bed frame so much that one night it collapsed, at a particularly dramatic moment. I guess enough was enough, even for a ghost. Had it not done so, my daughter might have been conceived on it instead of the floor-bound futon which, due to cheapness, laziness, and lingering mistrust of bed frames, became its heir.

No, Ilwan's ghost, if it existed, was the perfect roommate. And Ilwan wasn't alone: an attempt to paint-strip the doorframe shattered an old mezuzah, its tiny scroll of Torah quotations landing sacrilegiously on the floor among the paint fragments. (I reshrouded it in a Krazy Glue tube, and restored it to its guardian position.)

* * *

The neighborhood itself was well stocked with an array of freeloading spirits. Ethnoreligious ghosts: Second Avenue had been home to Yiddish theater, and the immigrant Jews who made it. Family ghosts: my father was born down on Madison, and his father and uncles had wandered those mean streets as entrepreneurs/hustlers whose involvement in small-time booze trafficking turned fatal for my grandfather. He died strung out after the boys upstairs ran heroin through their post-Prohibition distribution channels. Historical ghosts: the Commies from Union Square, the Socialists from the Forward building, the café where Trotsky sipped his borscht . . . Social ghosts of Beats, hippies, Yippies, punks, postpunks, and "white Negro" hipsters of every description—and the musical ghosts they hung out with: Albert Ayler playing "Bells" live at Slugs', Lee Morgan shot down on the street outside it.

I was on speaking terms with all the above, in particular the musical, whose history I imagined myself a part of. Actually, I imagined myself a part of all their histories, and much of my life consisted of this imagining. I *lived* "downtown," at the locus of these histories.

It took me a long time to realize that not everyone feels this way. But I don't think I was entirely alone in my imagining.

The inexhaustible reservoir of disappointment about the Lower East Side—the first "Downtown Is Dead" article appeared in the *Village Voice* in 1985—the seemingly endless ability of people to be shocked by its yuppification, this seemingly inexhaustible power to disappoint—is evidence of an equally inexhaustible hope.

This is the hope for History, with a capital H. That

thing that crawled off the boats from Europe along with "your tired, your poor." The Lower East Side was where history touched down, and where it stayed.

The -*nik* in beatnik refers back to Russian *narodniki*— the nineteenth-century idealistic Russian social movement whose romanticism became the bed of a historical river through which later narratives would flow, no matter how hard the Communists tried freeze it with cold dialectics.

The etymological punch of the word "yuppie," its sense of contradiction, comes from its position in a historical sequence: narodnik . . . Bolshevik, beatnik, hippie, Yippie . . . yuppie. It represents the final uncoiling of the spring of class tension from which that grand narrative derived.

It's not that so many of my fellow locus-dwellers were actual actual Leftists, just that these were the last Histories left, the last pillars propping up the whole wall. As LES poet Johnny Thunders would say, "And when they go, they let you know." What Thunders understood that all the Francis Fukuyama wiseasses don't is what it actually feels like to quit that habit.

In February 2005, I moved out.

"How do you like living in Brooklyn?" people ask.

I usually answer, as I'm supposed to: "It's great."

And why should it not be great?

My new apartment is bigger, not yet crammed to the ceiling with junk like the old place; it's one block from my daughter's school—no more frantic attempts to drag the poor kid onto the F train at seven thirty a.m.; it's on a quiet, properly residential block—I can give up the long and losing battle against my former neighbor: the groovy new Tuscan restaurant and their rocket-powered kitchen exhaust fans. The five-floor walk-up in Brooklyn is good for my legs. And yes, there are restaurants, museums, nightclubs here too. Even a few friends. Anyway, those friendships that couldn't survive the separation of five stops on the F train probably weren't very strong to begin with. Most importantly, my daughter now has her own bedroom (though probably shown in earlier schematics as a closet or bathroom, she, being small, finds it cozy and comfortable). This in turn creates the abstract possibility of my having a "social life," providing I someday overcome my inertia enough to arrange one, and stay off the road long enough to enjoy it.

"Brooklyn is great," I say, and everyone who either already lives here or is afraid they may have to because they're being priced out of Manhattan—that is to say, everybody I know—is relieved.

I only run into trouble when trying to describe, without sentimentality but with precision, what was lost in the move, so I usually don't bother.

But something was lost, and I miss it. Because I didn't change apartments: I never "lived" in that apartment on Second Avenue in the first place. I moved from a history into a "private life," from a locus to an address. My apartment grew; my world shrank.

The Lower East Side was always as much philosophic position as geographic location. To move "back" there (funny how even people whose parents weren't born there often describe moving "back") was to reverse the great American teleology of the westward expansion, toward nature, toward fortune and greatness, toward the heroic trial of the settlers' journey, toward a "manifest destiny." (No wonder so many people on the LES did junk: so much to negate, so little time.)

For Jews (especially the kind who wore black leather, played in punk bands, and never thought of themselves as Jews), this transgression went double.

Jacob Neusner, in *The Enchantments of Judaism*, argues that the practice of secularized American Jews (including all of us nonreligious quasi-Lefties who, maybe with some degree of irony, but "religiously" and without fail, do some kind of seder every Passover) represents not a less faithful practice based on the theology of "classical" Judaism, but a newer practice faithful to a newer theology of Holocaust (in Nazi Europe) and Redemption (in the State of Israel).

The "classical" tradition would consider anyone who doesn't believe in following Jewish law to be outside the framework of Judaism. The newer theology abandoned many of the practices called for by the law, and has given those it did retain different meaning. But by viewing the diaspora, the Holocaust, and the creation of the State of Israel as not simply historical but *theological* events, a teleology has been created: exile, diaspora, Holocaust, and Redemption in the State of Israel—from which its own adherents are excluded by virtue of the fact that we've actually chosen to remain in the US. (It ain't much of an "exile" if you can leave the vale of tears tomorrow and still have frequent flyer miles left over.)

Neusner wasn't writing particularly about Jewish musicians on the Lower East Side. But the effect of this schizoid situation on the artists of the Lower East Side is especially strong. By making art, we're contributing to a history. To whatever extent we're Jews, it's a Jewish history. To do this on the Lower East Side a big no-no. Because Jewish history isn't supposed to be happening here anymore: elsewhere, perhaps in the shtetls of the past (or among Hasids and other people who still look and talk like they live in them), during the Holocaust, in Israel maybe. But not here! Not now! Our lived history transgresses our teleology.

"Next year in Israel"—we roll our eyes through our chanting of this line at the end of every seder, having about as much intention of moving there as of jumping out the window, our irony neatly begging the question of where we *will* be next year. What we do hope. Who, and where in history, we are now.

A group of contemporary Jews who choose to remain in the US, didn't die in the Holocaust, aren't living in an imaginary shtetl or moving to Israel, who refuse (by continuing to create art) to behave as if we are in limbo: all this is an impossibility, a blasphemy (against a theology of Holocaust and Redemption). It shouldn't exist. It's history moving backward.

But at least it's moving.

If the LES is a philosophical position, why can't it be thought from Cobble Hill?

Well . . .

Because part of that position is about the way memory—and other thought—lives in objects. Jewish sacred text, for example, doesn't deal in metaphor, doesn't raise a crucified/signified son above the hollowed-out father/signifier, doesn't transform word into meat or meat into word: each word opens onto infinite signifiers through metonymy, yet remains simply what it is. The crown is also a heavy piece of metal. The land remains the land. The locus is also a place, a bar, a way of telling a bad joke, a worn-out avenue where the architectural remnants of theater marquees behind which soliloquies of a dead literature once rang out—and are still visible beneath the bank's renovated facade.

EPILOGUE

"In February 2005, I moved out."

Actually, the truth was a little more complicated.

When I was in my midtwenties to early thirties, before I moved to the Lower East Side, while playing guitar with the Lounge Lizards et al., I was also a volunteer tenant organizer with the Chelsea Coalition on Housing, a Met Council affiliate. I participated in a building occupation, went to court innumerable times, organized rent strikes, and helped put two criminal landlords in jail, a situation which involved sleeping with a baseball bat next to my bed for several years.

I was never a "leader"—those Communist tenant union ladies kicked ass, and I just tried to help. But after ten years of meetings, confrontations, living in an often-heatless mess of a 7A-administered building, my phone ringing every time some schmuck landlord didn't fix the boiler or tried to strong-arm the tenants, I moved out of the neighborhood, more than ready to return to civilian life. So when, during lease signing for that new pad on Second Avenue, the landlord let drop that it wasn't rent-stabilized, I raised my eyebrow but kept my mouth shut. Whatever.

Everything was cool for a while. The economy was bad, and the rent increases stayed roughly equivalent to what stabilization would have allowed anyway. And I was happy.

But in 1996, as I was nervously contemplating whether I was economically ready to handle my swiftly approaching fatherhood, the bastard sent me a lease jacking the rent by 40 percent. "You can't do this, it's a rent-stabilized apartment," I said.

"Is not," he said.

"Please don't do this," I begged him.

Ten years and about $170,000 of lost rent and wasted landlord attorney fees later, the landlord came around to my way of thinking. Actually, the original landlord didn't come around: he had died. But I settled with his widow.

Now I think it was unfair of this woman to imply, on the first of our two meetings, that I had killed her husband: with over twenty buildings in NYC, and an equal number in Florida, I doubt my level of annoyance was fatal. I'm sure he had lots of other reasons for drinking himself to death. It's a time-honored tradition in the former Soviet Republic of his birth. But since the good widow had chosen to introduce the issue of responsibility for her husband's death into our negotiations, I shared my belief that although I was humbly grateful if I had contributed in some small way, the honor was all hers.

Having thus clarified our positions, we quickly reached a deal: I moved out and dropped the court case; she tore up the bill for ten years of back rent, and made my lawyer happy.

As luck would have it, I had paid the rent money into an escrow account.

So now I'm living in a co-op in fashionable Cobble Hill, one block from Brooklyn's finest little public elementary school. The banks don't care how you buy your American dream, especially if you pay cash. Neither do my new neighbors and fellow co-operators. That I bought my yuppie respectability with the spoils of class war is just one of life's little ironies. It's all good with them, and I in turn sit at the board meetings and try to feel the passion they all seem to share about the issue of storm window replacement.

And you should see the view from my new roof-deck. All of downtown Brooklyn, a bit of the Verrazano Bridge to the south, the ferry-torn, gong-tormented waters of New York Harbor, giant cranes of the Red Hook Container Terminal, and all of Manhattan, stretched out at the erstwhile feet of the New York skyline's most famous absence.

Sometimes I really do feel lucky. After all, this is what millions risk drowning and imprisonment to achieve. I'm planning on running an electric line and some plumbing up there so I can put in a bar. "Up on the roof [deck]," beneath the immensity of the New York sky, surrounded by the city as aesthetic object, I can almost forget the feeling of waiting for something to happen.

Sometimes at night, my daughter and I watch the airplanes circle, lining up like impatient planets over Kennedy Airport. And sometimes, on a clear day, you can see all the way to New Jersey.

Today I Did Something Remarkable

Today I did something remarkable. I disassembled your loft bed, the one David Siegel and I had put together for you in 2006.

It had become inconvenient: the area underneath—so cozy when you were little—now too tiny, the space above too cramped, a relic of a childhood that no longer fit the young adult you've become.

Also, Uncle Jesse, tired of sleeping on the couch during visits, had been lobbying for a more adult-friendly compromise since you'd left. And so.

I looked into the timeless mess of my toolbox, and there (is there such a thing as a predictable miracle?) I found the strange IKEA Allen wrench (one of those monopoly tools that don't fit anything else) that I'd left there more than half your lifetime ago. It hadn't aged a bit.

It felt strange to be in the place where you'd experienced so much solitude, the chrysalis of your adolescence, navigating your things in your absence. You'd inherited my difficulty in parting with objects, so there was a lot to navigate—an archaeological palimpsest of new clothes, old tchotchkes, critical-theory texts, Legos, eyeliners, ancient radios, crayons—but eventually, I cleared a path to the necessary structural points of intervention.

Once freed of its mattress, the frame made reverb-y metallic sounds, like a David Van Tieghem percussion piece, or the score to one of your beloved horror movies.

I remembered buying the bed with you . . . and its predecessor in the Second Avenue apartment. It was one of the consolation prizes (the other was a cat, to which, unfairly and sadly, you later developed an allergy) for what you called "the divorce."

I don't know where you got the idea that loft beds were cool—but you got it. And you were right. I think it was Natalia who came up with the idea for the cute little desk underneath, the minidesign for your space-capsule-size room.

Moving to farther corners, I stumbled on funny things—the discs for the Reader Rabbit games that introduced you to reading (and apps)—and gross ones: oil-filled plastic buckets we'd placed around each leg of your bed during the bedbug horror were somehow still there, undergoing a yucky metamorphosis in the intervening eight years.

But it was a place made sacred by memory: the place where you laughed for hours with your friends from elementary and junior high (I remember being amazed at the ability of your girl gang to find so much happiness in such small places, without the punching, running, and breaking things of my own boyness) and hid to survive the terrible depression of your early high school years.

I remembered being annoyed at how long it always took to assemble our IKEA furniture, a task designed for geeks who just loved gluing model race cars or WW1 biplanes together all day (i.e.: not me).

But now I was grateful for the slowness of the task. Once yielding to pressure, the shiny machined pieces came apart as smoothly as when we had screwed them in. I worked in the silence of your room, undoing connection after connection, surrounded by memory, and by the objects of your memory. For a long time, my slow labor of undoing seemed to have no effect: the frame stayed as inexplicably solid as when I'd started, as if held in place by sheer force of habit, as if memory, for once, had defeated the laws of physics.

But finally I found the magic bolt, the one that had been holding everything together, and, midway through its unscrewing (as if borrowing a description from one of your childhood books), down it all came with a clatter.

Three Stories Involving Black Liquids

1.

So I walked to the Fairway in Red Hook, or the Gourmet Bazaar, or whatever they call it now. That's what I did . . . on days I did anything.

Most days I would decide to go out while there was still daylight, but then something would happen . . . I would start reading old e-mails, or fall asleep trying to study Italian. Or I would look for some piece of paper with something written on it and obsess about why I couldn't find it. Or maybe I couldn't find my keys, or my mask, or something. And so I just wouldn't make it outside.

But on the days when I did make it out of the house, it was usually almost twilight. This was only partly my fault. The days were short. It was winter.

It was a real winter too, a Brooklyn winter, with snow on the ground for months, turning fifty shades of gray outside the container terminal on the way to the Fairway or whatever it was. The checkout lady said, "It's just like winter in the old days." It was cold.

Going out late meant I didn't get any sun, which is bad for depression. (That was another thing I overheard in the checkout line at . . . let's just call it "the supermarket.")

But it had its own advantages. One is that there were fewer people, especially in the warehouse district of Red Hook, where there were never many people, even before. Fewer people with their germs.

And the other is that twilight always made me feel . . . something. Which is better than feeling nothing. I guess. If I got started too late, twilight itself could be too much, and I'd go home and eat my last can of beans, with some hot sauce and tamari. But if I got started earlier, the long twilight battle between electric and "natural" light made up for it. If I ever took pictures, I'd try to take pictures of that.

Anyway, it was a long walk to this particular supermarket, which is why I chose it. My mother told me on the phone, "It's bad to sit around the house all day. You'll get fat. You should get some exercise." Since she was ninety-three and lived in New Jersey, I figured she must know what she was talking about, so I did. By the time I reached my destination, it was always dark. Some people say that the darkest hour is always just before the dawn. I wouldn't know: I'm usually sleeping then. But I think the second-darkest hour must be just after twilight.

This particular supermarket had a steam table in the back, and a glass-enclosed eating area, which had somehow remained open even when all the other eating places were shut down, where you could eat your food out of the little take-out containers. I don't know why it was open. Maybe the pandemic inspectors overlooked it because they thought it was a supermarket. The food was bad, and it was almost always empty, but I liked it. I developed a kind of ritual: when I was finished shopping, I'd get some grilled tilapia or chicken and eat it in the enclosed area with a ginger ale. When it was light out, you could see New York Harbor. Even when it was pitch-black out, it was nice to know that a scenic harbor was out there somewhere.

And it made me feel normal to eat in a restaurant, even if it wasn't really a restaurant. Which shows how little it takes to make someone feel normal. But which I guess also shows how little it takes to make someone stop feeling normal.

Unfortunately, this particular visit didn't go as planned. When I finished my shopping, the steam table was closed. I bought my ginger ale and a take-out sushi dish . . . but when I tried to go out the usual door into the dining area, it was locked. "Why?" I asked the cashier.

She said the people who ran the supermarket decided to close earlier.

"Now where am I going to eat this sushi?" I asked.

She shrugged, said I couldn't have my money back, and went back to lacquering her nails.

I rolled my shopping cart to the front of the store, where I had to check out a second time, putting my supply of beans, anchovies, and sardines into my backpack. I didn't like those foods. But I was supposed to eat them because they don't have cholesterol, and I liked vegetables even less. The delicate balance I had maintained through twilight was gone, and I became aware of a deep void below. I thought of the Auden line: *A crack in the tea kettle opens / a lane to the land of the dead.* Things hadn't ended well for Auden.

The supermarket was closing. The marquee lights were off. Men in soiled white jackets were collecting shopping carts from the parking lot, banging them together into long trains, locking them with cables. It was colder. Somehow, there was a metal table and chair at the edge of the parking lot, near wooden crates and unmarked bags and boxes.

I sat down, fearful that the cart men might evict me at any moment. I took the plastic cover off my sushi, smeared the little plastic fish's stingy portion of wasabi onto the California rolls, and tried to open the soy sauce packet. It wouldn't open. There was a tiny arrow on the packet, but I couldn't figure out what it meant. I tried my teeth, and met incredible resistance, even though I gnawed like a hungry rat. The cart men were getting closer. I tried to calm myself . . . Surely millions of people who eat take-out sushi all over the world don't freak out over a fucking soy sauce packet. There must be some meaning to the arrow, some tiny indentation that I was missing, something every fucking sushi-eating idiot in the world could see right away but I was too stupid to learn.

Then it happened, like god's grace descending on the sinner—the entire packet squirted onto my hands and the sleeve of my overcoat. I sat there looking at my palms. Two supermarket men were approaching.

2.

In 1970s Europe, far-left guerrilla groups like the Italian Brigate Rosse carried out a series of what they called "attentats" (and most of the media called "terrorism") intended to "heighten the contradictions of capitalism" by pushing liberal "bourgeois democracies" into ever more repressive action. They succeeded in this goal, but the repression failed to ignite the popular revolution they had hoped for. And, so, the would-be revolutionaries were eventually rounded up, imprisoned, killed, exiled, or driven to suicide.

This is a time I remember well, because the manhunts leading to the final arrests were active during my first tour of Europe in 1979—with the late jazz organist Brother Jack McDuff. Apparently, I was a dead ringer for a German revolutionary whose photo on posters at every European border control didn't yet have a little *X* (meaning: *captured*) over it. McDuff was very amused to see the border police tormenting a white person for a change: while the agents poked at my papers and dissected my luggage, he and the drummer, a tall fellow from Chicago named Garyck who wore a coke spoon as a necklace, would stand at a safe distance smiling with delight.

Anyway, it was all over long ago, and I have no idea what, if anything, it meant. But the legacy of the Brigate Rosse, the Baader-Meinhof Gang, et al., lives on in the European regulations requiring every hotel to record the passport or residency card data of every guest.

That, and some combination of my own and a hotel clerk's forgetfulness, is why I missed my flight from Graz, Austria, to Bologna, Italy, one morning in the early '90s.

I had checked into the hotel the day before, surrendering my passport as requested, and gone immediately to Graz's famously progressive architectural institute, where someone had convinced me to give a talk. *But I don't know anything about architecture*, I had written back from NYC. *I'm going to crawl on my hands and knees and bark like a dog.*

Great! my sponsor had replied, without a trace of irony, before offering more money than I usually made in a week.

I did some barking in the actual performance, but this

was juxtaposed with guitar improvisation using extended techniques, noise elements, atonality, polytonality, intercut with fragments of jazz standards, heavy metal tunes, nursery rhymes, and spoken-word descriptions of buildings I liked. You know: "downtown."

Apparently, the performance's structure—or lack of it—had something to do with what the institute's architects were designing. They clapped politely at the end, and the sponsor presented me with a bottle of the pumpkin seed oil known as Kernöl, considered a great delicacy in Styria.

I was driven to the airport the following morning, my ticket processed by an attractive blond woman in the pale-blue Austrian Airlines uniform.

My reverie on the fetish power of uniforms was interrupted by her routine request for a passport. It wasn't in its usual place, and an image of the hotel clerk (a pasty-faced old night porter whose demeanor suggested earlier employment at nearby Theresienstadt) requesting it the day before flashed back.

As I ransacked my luggage hoping to be proven wrong, the check-in agent confirmed that even if the hotel sent the passport by taxi immediately, I would miss my flight to Bologna. There were no other flights till late that evening.

I sprang into disjointed action, changing dollars into schillings, buying a phone card, yelling at the hotel clerk on my mobile phone, researching train connections and car rentals, trying to reach the Italian singer-songwriter whose recording session I was about to miss, dragging my mess of luggage and guitars back and forth in the provincial airport— all under the gaze of airline personnel whose initial compassion with my misfortune was quickly fading.

My carry-on bag was made of black canvas, the type then used by bicycle messengers, with a main compartment filled with various things, and a smaller zippered lid. During one of many frantic searches through little pieces of paper and itineraries, I flipped back the top compartment, forgetting that it contained the bottle of Kernöl—until I heard the muffled crunch of glass.

After a moment of frozen panic, I set off for the men's room at top speed, leaving drops of greenish-black oil in an accelerating trail on the shiny airport floor.

The disapproving eyes of the woman in the pale-blue Austrian Airlines uniform followed me from her unmoving face.

Luckily, the Herren's was vacant and there were paper towels there for the grabbing. The main compartment of the black bag contained important papers—plane tickets, books, diary, phone numbers—in the process of immersion by the spreading flood of Kernöl.

I amputated the top of my bag in triage.

Had someone entered the men's room at that moment, they would have seen me on my knees leaning into the toilet stall, surrounded by mounds of wadded paper towels and shards of glasss, smears and splatters of greenish-black liquid covering the stall and everything in it, hacking feverishly at a mysterious wet object like a sweating psycho-killer butchering a Martian.

Fortunately, no one witnessed my crime.

3.

What can I say about Micki?

That I loved her the way only a nineteen-year-old having his first real relationship after moving out of his parents' house can love a twenty-eight-year-old woman? That the sight of a discarded pair of her cutoffs gave me a hard-on? That she looked a little bit like the drawing of Joni Mitchell on the cover of *Clouds*? That our love sang of utopia and redemption . . . ? That she was crazy, controlling, and deluded? That things ended badly, with me running into the frigid Augusta night wearing only a T-shirt to hitchhike to NYC, my hand bloody from having punched out the storm window? That she died in 2009, having spent a number of the intervening years harassing me by telephone and sleeping on other people's couches to avoid homelessness?

In 1975, I followed Micki from Boston to South Hope, Maine (or No Hope, as we came to call it during the first winter, with ever-diminishing irony), but I would have followed her anywhere. I know that's a cliché. But it was true for me at the time.

I had been thirteen years old during New York's version of the Summer of Love, and had fallen in love, hopelessly, impossibly, with the young hippie women I'd seen smiling, beatifically stoned at demonstrations, the Donovan concert in Central Park, in Washington Square where I'd have picnics with my aunt and guitar teacher after my Sunday-morning lessons. I was in love with all of them, in love with the beautiful moment that seemed to be happening. I knew the moment wouldn't last. I knew the young women wouldn't wait, frozen in time, till I was old enough . . . but I literally prayed that they would.

I met Micki through a friend from the food co-op movement with whom I'd worked as a part-time freelance banana truck unloader at Boston's Chelsea wholesale market after dropping out of Boston University. It was a great job—started around four a.m., finished by seven or eight, leaving the whole day free. And it paid fifteen dollars a truck: a lot considering that the rent for my part of an apartment on the Roxbury side of Mission Hill was forty dollars a month.

If the banana work was slow, I could make a deposit at the blood bank, another easy twenty dollars (you were only supposed to do it once a month, but no one checked; the winos in the waiting room told me they did it every day). And there was always the Handy Andy Industrial Temporary Help Services in the downtown "Combat Zone," or stealing stripped copper from vacant buildings with my more entrepreneurial colleagues.

At the time, I could eat for five to seven dollars a week, thanks to the Mission Hill Food Co-op (formerly the Mission Hill People's Revolutionary Food Co-op, and conceived as a community-organizing project) for which I volunteered as a grain buyer, and through whose wholesaler connections I got the banana truck gig.

My banana-unloading friend Ben was living at the communal house of a rival (the less radical Boston Food Co-op), a sprawling, comfortable, dilapidated old place with seemingly infinite rooms, perched at the top of a steep Jamaica Plain street.

What Micki was doing there was a bit hazy. But a similar fog enveloped many others in that place and time. Apparently, she had left Maine on her way to join a commune in Tennessee, ran out of money in Boston, was attempting to replenish it by working as an art model, and in the meantime decided not to go to Tennessee.

Banana-truck Ben also played guitar, and I met Micki when he invited me over to the Boston Food Co-op house to jam. There were so many people hanging around that Micki and I had been having sex for a week before I figured out that the cute curly-haired four-year-old named David was actually hers, and the bearded guy living with his girlfriend one floor up was her husband.

But it was cool. David liked it when I read him books or we drew pictures together. Jon wasn't jealous or anything. He got me a job at the furniture-repair place he was working in JP, and sold me a VW Bug he'd fixed up for next to nothing.

One day, while we were stopped at a traffic light on the way to work, he peered at me with a strange expression and said, "Umm, maybe we should talk about Micki."

I didn't want to hear it. I got defensive and said, "I really love her, man," glaring into his eyes like Charlie Manson on the cover of *Life*.

"Yeah," he sighed, and looked away. The light changed.

In the spring, Micki decided to move back up to Maine. I'm not sure why. I guess there was more nature there. Or cities were bad for kids. Or something. More worldly participants in the "back to the land" movement had figured out that before we "get ourselves back to the Garden," we should try to buy one, or make sure we knew someone who had. Maine in the 1970s was competing with Alabama for the position of "poorest state in the Union." Friendly rich people were hard to come by. And although there were plenty of gardens, there turned out to be no jobs that paid or lasted long enough for us to buy one. Anyway, planning wasn't really our strong suit. It wasn't just that we were a little bit dumb and smoked a lot of weed. The latter, at least, was more effect than cause. It was like we were waiting for something BIG to happen, something that would leap out of history like a beast in the jungle and, for better or worse, make our personal plans superfluous. It just took us a little longer than most people to figure out that it never would.

All our possessions fit in the VW with room to spare. David was propped in the back with his toy monkey, next to my guitar, blankets, and big bags of food co-op grain. Jon was standing on the stoop smoking a pipe. I went back into the house for a last item, a precious gallon jug of tamari. As I was handing it to Micki to put in the car, one of us slipped, and the glass jar shattered, gushing a river of tamari down the steep hill, its receding black wave staining the sidewalk into the distance. We knew this was a portent, but didn't yet know of what. We watched in silence till the black streak disappeared into Columbus Avenue, then said our goodbyes, leaving Jon to sweep up the broken glass, and drove north.

I Terremotati

The first time I felt an earthquake was in Los Angeles. I was there for rehearsals. It was morning when the shaking began, and I determined not to die in the shitty La Brea motel where the road manager stuck us. The motel desk clerk had shifty eyes, the housekeeper stole some cash from my suitcase, and I didn't trust the people who designed, built, and inspected the place either. In fact, I didn't trust LA itself (and still don't). I ran past the astroturf deck chairs and plastic ferns around the mini-pool, the cheap laminations of the lobby bar, and into the sunlight. The shaking had passed. A pack of construction workers laughed at the rattled New Yorker standing in his underwear and T-shirt. They were used to such things.

The second time was in Tokyo. I was on tour with the Lounge Lizards in the mid '80s, on the twenty-third floor of the Roppongi Prince Hotel, looking out the window, talking to my long-distance girlfriend . . . barely noticing a vibration like the familiar rattling of my West 16th Street apartment—till it inched into my consciousness that thirty-story buildings don't shake like rotten-beamed tenements when trucks go by. This time I didn't panic. In fact, the earthquake reminded me of the Magic Fingers bed in an Atlantic City hotel where my family had stayed when I was a kid. It was nice. Mildly pornographic. *Relaxing*, as it said above the Magic Fingers coin slot. The only troubling thing at all was the thought, purely intellectual, that a half hour later I might be a hand protruding from the rubble in some Tokyo bureau AP photo.

Another time I felt an earthquake was in Trieste, Italy, when I was waking up in the apartment of my partner (I was older now, and didn't feel comfortable saying "girl-friend"; and anyway, this wasn't the same person to whom I'd told the Magic Fingers story). She'd gone to work, and I was still lying in bed. This time the quake was slower, more like pulsation than vibration. The cat leaped off my stomach and glared with hard suspicion from the floor. A wooden mannequin of Pinocchio shook off the bookshelf and broke. I decided we should try to live, but by the time I grabbed the cat and moved to shelter in the doorframe . . . it had stopped.

It was nothing really, for us.

Seven people had died near Zagreb.

Italians have words for those traumatized by earth-quakes: *i terremotati*. Etymologically, it derives from *terre* (earth) and *mutati* (changed): *those changed by the earth*.

The earthquakes come more often now, although they're rarely mentioned on the news. Perhaps there are more im-portant disasters to discuss. Or maybe I've become more sensitive. I lie awake in the middle of the night and feel it shaking. Sometimes in the afternoon too. Even in parts of the city where there are no subways. Sometimes it seems as if the trembling will never stop.

Part III

FILM (MIS)TREATMENTS

Party Boat
[unfilmable treatment #1]

All dialogue will be direct quotations from the script of *Titanic*. In particular, the dialogue of 1) the central lover; and the subplots of 2) the doomed musicians/trendy party dancers; and 3) the increasingly nervous ship's officers, will be isolated from the rest of the script and quoted at length, while all other subplots and their attendant dialogue will be dropped. Dialogue, even (or especially) if out of context, will be repeated more or less verbatim.

There will, however, be several critical alterations in the scenario: in our version, the boat never leaves the dock, which is the pier near le Jet d'Eau in Lac de Genève. Also, rather than hitting an iceberg, our boat's engine falls out because the boat is rotten. Our boat is also a bit smaller than the *Titanic*: it is a Lac de Genève excursion boat. It nevertheless sinks slowly enough to deliver all the dialogue needed. In our version, the sinking can be even slower than the original, with much of it taking place with the actors increasingly engulfed in water.

The tragic sinking and deaths occur against a backdrop of a sunny spring afternoon on the Lac de Genève pier, of random people strolling, bicycling, pushing baby carriages along the quay to which the boat is docked, approximately three feet behind the boat's port side. Since the main deck of the boat is slightly below pier level, these people are visible, except for babies and dogs, only from the waist down.

At intervals during the film—determined entirely by the Fibonacci sequence—we cut to the heroic profile of a handsome man in traditional Swiss costume framed by a clear blue sky, his hand cupped to his mouth, shouting, "Le Jet d'Eau!" followed by a brief interlude in which all the actors stop to gaze rapturously at an eruption of le Jet d'Eau, accompanied by wondrous harp arpeggios, and then, in unison, resume whatever they were doing previously.

We can do away with all the character-development parts: they're boring, and besides, everyone already saw the original. Our version begins with the scene culminating in the male lead holding the female lead up at the front of the ship to experience LIFE. Except, of course, since the boat isn't moving and there's no wind, there's not that much to experience.

As the boat goes down, the doomed musicians stoically play a mix of classical music themes, standards, and greatest hits from the Marc Ribot songbook, including such memorable tunes as "White People Find Each Other Attractive (Yes They Do)," "The Empire State Building," "Yo, I Killed Your God," etc., while the dancers do the Frug and the Madison.

The "redemptive" end of the film is omitted. In this version, no one escapes drowning: there are no life rafts, and no one knows how to swim, or has much of a desire to learn. More significantly, no one can be bothered to reach for the pier, even though it's only a few feet away.

Three-Star Desperadoes
(or, Biting the Hand)

Cast of Characters:

The no-wave band (the Kings of Modern Jazz), consisting of:

—*a female violinist or guitarist:* Gail (grouchy, lesbian)

—*male electric organ player:* Frank (intellectual, gay, aristocratic pretensions)

—*male (?) drummer:* Jesús (Puerto Rican/deep South Bronx)

—*male guitarist (Jewish):* Bob (deep Brooklyn, hustler/used-car-salesman characteristics)

—*transgender singer/sax player:* Mr. Fashion

All the above are mildly depressed.

The sexual dynamics of the band are such that no intraband romance is likely. In fact, they're a collection of ethnic/gender/class differences and temperamental polarities who nevertheless like each other, to a point, and share a long history. A weird dysfunctional (and weirdly dysfunctional) family (i.e., a band).

—*the manager:* Arthur (eternally exasperated straight white guy)

—*the inspector:* Inspector Clouseau type.

—*elusive dumpling master:* Chef Ho

—various attractive waiters, waitresses, cooks, and maître d's

This is a tale of two clichéd genres. Content, wherever possible, should be lifted from the following sources:

1) Contemporary writing on haute cuisine, restaurant criticism, the *Michelin Guide*, cookbooks, television cooking shows, etc. Restaurant scenes have the feeling of cinema verité documentary footage, the culinary equivalent of a fishing show. It should embellish on the contemporary writing, going further into aesthetic criticism of the visuals (a seven-course meal in which the *amuse-gueule* at the beginning, a warm quail egg yolk surrounded by cold, well-beaten egg whites, served in a white half-eggshell, foreshadows the white porcelain cup of coffee at the end). Criticism of the food as text is also welcome: interesting to invite postmodern theorists Fredric Jameson (is he alive?) or Paul Harvey, or poststructuralists like Žižek, to share "research" meals and then write short bits, or even film them expounding on the meals eaten in the film.

2) Famous gunfighting scenes. These scenes are pure action movie, and each should reference a particular gun battle in another film. Exactly which film/director is determined by which can be most closely linked to the particular cuisine in the preceding scene. For example, a dining scene at Lucas Carton in Paris, which features subtle fusion with Oriental cuisine, could be followed by a John Woo gun battle. The scene following the restaurant Can Fabes outside Barcelona could reference the shootout from *The Good, the Bad, and the Ugly*, etc. The above genres are set within a third: a type of road movie. Overall, the camerawork, like

the musical score, should not necessarily be amateurish or low-budget, but, like no-wave music, should privilege the aesthetic of cheapness.

The "story" takes place in the present:

The Kings of Modern Jazz are an avant-garde outfit who were critics' darlings about fifteen years ago. Since that time, however, the critics have gone elsewhere, and any enthusiasm the musicians might have once felt toward music (and this is somewhat in doubt, since they may have always viewed it as a hustle or an annoying job) has completely disappeared, replaced by a fanatical obsession with food. Their obsession, while focused on haute cuisine and the never-ending task of securing reservations at three-star *Michelin Guide* restaurants, is poststructuralist enough to encompass the pleasures of cheap but excellent dumpling houses and unusually good hot dogs, egg creams, knishes. Their dialogue consists mostly of comparisons, critiques, and reminiscences about these food experiences.

The film begins as the band is preparing for their twentieth-anniversary European tour. The manager has begged them to write new material, rehearse. He's seen on the phone lining up concerts, promising the promoters that although the band hasn't put out a new record in eight years, they're sounding great, that this project is really new, improved, exciting, etc. The band, meanwhile, is meeting at Chef Ho's Dumpling House, planning their own culinary shadow itinerary, arguing over which restaurant to eat at in each city they play, adjusting the logistics by deciding to cancel sound checks and telling the manager to make concert times later/earlier, and so on.

When the food arrives, they taste it, only to be disappointed—this clearly isn't the work of their friend, the brilliant Chef Ho. They demand to see Ho, find out that in fact he's no longer there, get in a big argument with the staff (culminating perhaps in a food fight—foreshadowing the more violent conflicts to come), leave traumatized. (The mystery of the disappearance of Chef Ho is a subplot reappearing periodically during the film.)

On tour in Europe, the band's years of resting on their laurels catches up with them. The band's degeneration is represented by their sounding like a no-wave band. The crowd boos (Euro/serious-jazz-festival ambience). The band barely notices. They have dinner plans. But a solemn-faced manager interrupts them in the dressing room with bad news. He reads them some choice quotes from a ream of scathing reviews. The band laughs. He finally gets their attention with the announcement that the rest of the concert dates have been canceled. He's canceling all the travel arrangements and booking them on a flight back home the next day. The band understand this also means the cancelation of their meticulously planned restaurant tour.

They beg the manager not to cancel the travel arrangements. He persists. They argue. A fight ensues, during which they kill him. The killing should be clumsy, as in an amateur film, without enough foreshadowing in the score to make it truly violent: he gets bopped on the head with an instrument case, and voilà!—he's dead.

The reaction of the band is also understated: "Oh my, he's dead. Yuck."

The band quickly decide to take advantage of the situation; to continue the tour, simply omitting the concerts.

This plan works perfectly. Montage of tourist shots/ happy eating scenes in the great cities of Europe. The ambience of the restaurant scenes isn't the cold, disdainful spectacle of American film haute cuisine; the actual contemporary reality is relaxed, friendly—the restaurant staff are artists who take pride in their creations. They recognize the band's (food) expertise and are happy to respond to questions. Surprisingly, no one is critical of the fact that in every other aspect of dress, speech, and behavior, the band seems totally out of place in the expensive restaurant settings.

However, the band quickly run out of money. This becomes critical after a detailed, extended restaurant scene. The food is great. The band chats (occasionally in French) with the friendly waiters. The atmosphere is warm . . . but after the meal, a slightly embarrassed head waiter returns: "*Pardonnez-moi, monsieur, il y a un petit problème avec votre carte de credit . . .*" The moment of truth has arrived. The maître d' threatens to call the police. The band whip out guns and start shooting. The restaurant staff, who all turn out to be well-armed, transform instantly into the band's rival in a John Woo gangster movie gun battle. Finally, after protracted and extreme violence, the band wins (or at least escapes). They all take mints and cards on the way out.

This basic scene is repeated in various other major European cities, the change in venues allowing for a discussion of the various national cuisines. Relations with the staff are usually amicable before the bloodbath. (An exception, in which the staff cop an attitude, provides a variation.) In London, a hip young chef takes them into the kitchen to demonstrate cooking techniques. When they have to shoot him later, it'll hurt them more than it'll hurt him.

The restaurant scenes are interspersed with travel scenes, a sort of vacant road movie in which the boredom of travel serves as a backdrop for slow character exposition. Travel should, in the beginning, be by train. A variation could be provided by having the group steal a delivery van (with some obvious product-placement logo on the side) as part of an escape after a shootout. The driving sequences could also allow for some roadside food adventures—for example, a tapas bar (called "Bar") filled with hostile locals in the middle of nowhere in spaghetti-western country outside Madrid.

The exposition and dialogue gradually reveal the empty lives of the more or less unsympathetic characters—failed romances, aborted attempts at normality, Beat solipsism—lives which, beneath the no-longer-opaque surface of their professionalism, read like an inversion of the idea of human potential.

Example:

Jesús: "Hey Gail, you ever have, you know, like a relationship . . . like a steady girlfriend . . . ?"

Gail: "Nah."

Bob [after a pause]: "No? What about that girl Zoey you were goin' out with for a while?"

Gail: "Eh, she was okay, but in the end, just couldn't trust her."

Bob: "Really? You two seemed pretty hot for a while. Shit, you must have been with her at least a couple of years, right?"

Gail: "Look, I'd rather not talk about it, okay?"

Bob: "Oh c'mon. I remember she was devastated when you two split up, seems like I was tripping over her in every bar in the East Village for months. Whatever happened with you two?"

Gail: "Fuck. You really want to know? Okay. If you ask me, love is a bunch of shit. I mean, just when you think you can really trust somebody, they stab you in the back, just like that. I did everything for that girl. I was really there for her. Everything. Then, remember our tour of Japan in '88?"

All: "Yeah."

Gail: "One little thing I ask her. One little thing: take care of Goldie and Swimmie."

Jesús: "Wha?"

Gail: "Goldie and Swimmie, my goldfish. You remember!"

Jesús: "Uh."

Gail [who shows almost no emotion during the rest of the film, becomes agitated to the point of tears during the following]: "I gave her the food, I wrote out instructions. 'Not too much,' I said. I showed her. I made her practice in front of me. 'Not too little. But not too much. Just enough. Just this much. Two little pinches for Goldie, two for Swimmie. Otherwise it hurts their tummies.' She said she understood, and I trusted her, that bitch."

Bob, Jesús [increasingly horrified reaction shots]: "What did she do?"

Gail: "Nothing, that's what she did. She didn't do shit! And when I came home, what did I find? My Swimmie was dead. Dead . . . floating on her poor little side at the top of the tank." *[She cries.]* "And we used to have so much fun. 'Come to

Momma,' I'd say, and she would hear me, and give a little swim around the tank just for me. And I swear, she would come up to the glass and give me little kisses. My Swimmie . . ." *[sobs openly]*

Bob [horror and disbelief]: "You mean you left Zoey over a fish?"

Gail: "I loved that fucking fish . . ."

[Bob and Jesus react with faint nausea.]

Frank [bursting into train compartment]: "Get ready, boys and girls, we're almost in Strasbourg! We'll have ten minutes to make La Tour d'Argent in time for lunch."

[General excitement, hubbub. Cut to exterior, frantically throwing bags off train, running for cabs. Music: "Don't Want to Be Happy" (James Chance and the Contortions). *"I only live on the surface, I don't think people are very pretty inside . . ."*]

With each character, at the point when the viewer begins to beg for less exposition, the enthusiasm for food brings the characters (and the film) back to life.

An element of suspense is introduced: an inspector is on their trail.

The inspector, though incredibly inept, eventually closes in, finally matching the sites of the crimes with the group's tour itinerary.

The gig's up.

Desperate and hungry, with the police closing in, the band are saved by their old friend Chef Ho, who appears miraculously out of nowhere with an offer to lead them to freedom . . . if they can make a deal.

Final scene is set somewhere in a remote, rural corner

of a Special Economic Zone in China, at Chef Ho's Lakeside Hideaway, a sort of Chinese Catskills resort. Chef Ho is stirring a bowl of something in front of the restaurant. A sign reads (in Chinese): *Real American Jazz.* Ho talks directly to the camera, interview style, delivering a sober critique of no-wave music:

"Let's face it, the sense of urgency that was so palpably present on their records from the early '80s just isn't there anymore. I mean, at that time, they really had something to say about the state of jazz. And there was an audience capable of hearing it then too. Both had come out of a moment when jazz, contemporary classical, and avant/punk rock appeared to meet at a sort of a crossroads. Some of it sounds silly now, but I think their reinterpretation of Monk is still really valid—and god, if only the so-called young lions had a glimmer of their appreciation for how boring their automatic modernism sounds. Jeez . . . Okay, I admit, by the mid-'90s, the compositional tricks began to feel a bit like shtick, and in fact, they were never contenders in the chops department. But on a good night, they still really have this—well, you can't quite call it swing, but it's something. Yeah, I would say it's definitely something."

[During this speech a band is beginning to play in the other room, getting louder toward the end—a raving no-wave version of "Moonlight Serenade."]

Then: roll credits. Eventually, Elvis Costello's "Radio, Radio" plays, beginning on the line: *"I wanna bite the hand that feeds me, I wanna bite that hand so badly . . ."*

Hungry: A Thirty-Minute Real-Time One-Take Disaster Film

John, Deborah, and Harry are going to the city by train. They really want to eat sandwiches before they go, but they don't have time. Now they're really hungry. Whose fault is it? Each blames the other. As the journey progresses, they become increasingly hungry and irritable, then angry and desperate, till they finally have no choice but to resort to cannibalism.

They eat Harry.

(This takes place on the NJ Transit Midtown Direct train between South Orange, New Jersey, and Penn Station in Manhattan. The entire trip takes thirty minutes. Soon after the act of cannibalism, the conductor announces *Penn Station*, and John and Deborah walk off into the crowded station, past bars and fast-food places, and into the sunlight of Seventh Avenue.)

Note: Harry doesn't really protest being killed and eaten. He understands. After all, it had to be somebody. None of the other commuters, although annoyed, are bothered enough to put down their newspapers.

Dialogue of the Sushi Eaters

Location: Japanese restaurant exactly like Osaka on Court Street, across from Cobble Hill Cinemas in Brooklyn.

Scenario: The camera follows as the subject enters the restaurant. Three sushi chefs in identical white outfits greet the subject from behind the sushi counter at the far end of the long rectangular room. Seven or eight people, some in couples, some alone, are dining naturalistically, scattered among various tables.

The camera scans the room. There is no music, and most of the couples are silent . . . The waitresses take orders.

Food arrives and is eaten.

Eventually, someone gets up to go to the bathroom.

The bathroom is in the basement, down a long flight of steep wooden stairs, the door to which is just to the left of the sushi counter. As the bathroom-goer approaches the door, the camera pans down to reveal that one of their shoelaces is untied.

The camera cuts between shots of the sushi chefs (who are all looking, silently and impassively, at the untied shoelace) from the POV of the bathroom-goer, and shots of the approaching untied shoelace from the perspective of the main sushi chef; accompanied by a *Jaws*-like score of menacing, repetitive riffs building in speed, volume, and intensity, until the bathroom-goer enters the basement stairway and closes the door behind them.

The click of the door is followed, after a beat, by the sound of a body falling down the flight of stairs.

Camera remains on the impassive faces of the sushi chefs as they hear this sound. A few beats go by in silence. Then one of the sushi chefs wearily walks over to the basement door and enters the stairway, the door closing behind him. You hear his feet descending the staircase, the sound of a body being dragged, a grunt, the sound of a body landing on a floor, and the sound of another door being shut.

You then hear steps ascending the stairs.

The sushi chef reappears from behind the door, and resumes his place behind the counter.

None of the other diners appear to have heard the sound of the falling body, or, if they have, they don't react in any way. Even the dining partner of the former bathroom-goer doesn't seem surprised at their nonreturn.

Eating/serving/silence/light-talking go on as before . . . until someone else gets up to go to the bathroom and the preceding sequence repeats itself.

The sequence repeats itself for each person in the restaurant, till there is no one left.

Following this, the sushi chefs and the waitress stand still, silently staring around or in the direction of the camera for three minutes.

Finally, one walks over to the door to the basement stairs, and, with a hammer, nails a piece of paper to it. The piece of paper says:

If you are going to the bathroom,
Please tie your shoes.

The sushi chef then resumes his position with the other two sushi chefs, with the bored waitress to the side.

Camera dollies backward, and exits the restaurant.

The End

Death in Venus

Death in Venus: a science fiction rewrite of *Death in Venice, E.T.*, and the Christopher Columbus story.

An aging (*My Favorite Martian* type) Martian bisexual who had been attempting to travel to Venus gets terribly lost and crash-lands on Earth, in the water near Venice.

After swimming ashore, he walks around Venice believing himself to be on Venus, stalks a young bratty American tourist, and dies.

The soundtrack would be entirely constructed: mostly scary theremin sounds and noise guitar. No dialogue, no live recording. A few matting effects—waves, crowd sounds, individuals—match the visuals, but highly processed (distorted, pitch-shifted an octave down, chorused, flanged, maybe harmonized?), as mimesis of the sound heard by nonhuman eardrums; as mimesis of "alienation."

Will it play in Peoria? Who knows! But it's no less plausible than Christopher Columbus mistaking Jamaica for Goa— and they bought that, right?

The Club-Date
Musician (or, Saturday
Night Nausea)

This film takes place circa 1978, and centers around the
life of an alienated wedding band musician named Max,
a young saxophonist who, while dreaming of and to some
extent working toward a truly new music, supports himself
by playing "club dates," the NYC term for the wedding/bar
mitzvah circuit.

The film has a minimal narrative structure, based on
several plots:

1) Max's problematic relation with his employer, Nat
Alexander (all club-date orchestra leaders have two first
names, always both Waspy, and almost all are Jews or Italians or both), who he discovers is paying kickbacks for referrals
and the exclusion of rival orchestras—and may have participated in the violent shakedown of other bandleaders—when
he takes too long to pack up at the end of a gig, and inad-
vertently overhears an argument involving Alexander and
the Mafia caterer. Max now "knows too much," and the
Mafia guy wants Alexander to fire him—or worse. Alexander
pretends he has, meanwhile simply farming him out to gigs in
other catering halls . . . but there is tension about discovery.

2) Max's relationship with his girlfriend. Although apparently weighted down with the problems of young broke people in NYC, the real problem is this: Max, whose job is playing at weddings, can't marry. He's haunted by the image of assembly-line weddings (at Leonard's of Great Neck, the Huntington Town House, and other NYC-area wedding factories), and can't construct the myth of uniqueness necessary for marriage. Max contrasts his mother's idyllic description of her wedding to Max's father, her wonder at the fact they had "a swan made of ice," with his experienced knowledge that anyone can have a swan made of ice (it's in the catalog for $350), and the behind-the-scenes brutality that went into making it and the rest of the genteel wedding experience (maître d's in the "colonial room," screaming at the Mexican employees: "Get those fuckin' flowers on the table, you Puerto Rican bastards!" seconds before opening the door with a smile to the gowned and tuxedoed guests.)

The film is a tour of the NYC wedding industry subculture through Max's eyes: the platform where brides stand to show off their dresses, automatically revolving around like cakes in a diner pastry window; the "chapel" at Huntington Town House, with its button to make the crucifix disappear into the wall while the eternal light rolls out. And, more specifically, the wedding-band industry, with its weird infrastructure of club-date offices, sending out bands that the customers all think are the same, but which, if they're lucky, may contain only one member of the band they thought they were hiring, bands which never rehearse but are able to get by, more or less via lowest-common-denominator arrangements of a standard repertoire.

There's also exposition of the musicians' special language: a "screamer" is a wedding in which not even one member of the band the wedding party thought they were hiring is present. ("Get there early, it's a screamer.") Various anecdotes can be incorporated: What happens when somebody dies at a club date in NYC? The band plays "Hava Nagila" really fast until the catering staff can erect a scaffolding to hide the corpse. Various characters are introduced: the bitter old former big-band serious bebop guitarist, forced to play "Jeremiah Was a Bullfrog" with a wah-wah pedal, packing venom and disgust into each mechanical *wah*.

But the real narrative of the film is the life and death of Max's illusion that he can be "in it but not of it," both in terms of love and art; that he can maintain an impermeable wall protecting his dream from the world in which he lives every day; and Max's growing breakdown as that wall shatters.

This narrative becomes evident through the relation between the background score and the foreground "source music." At the beginning of the film, Max is heard in the source music doing his job well, playing wedding music as it should be played, perhaps even tastefully. The score, however, presents the music Max is hearing in his head, the music he is dreaming toward, but because of lack of funding and connections—and more fundamentally, an ambivalence about compromise with the world that *any* realization of art entails—is unable to get played.

As the film and Max's disillusionment progress, he begins to play increasingly "out" during the club dates, and bits of wedding-band kitsch start to bleed into the score.

Finally, score and source music invert entirely: the score

is entirely Muzak—and this background music, incorporated toward the end of the film, grows increasingly loud and distorted. Meanwhile, Max plays with complete disregard for club-date conventions, blowing his brains out on the sax—oblivious to the horrified wedding/bar mitzvah guests—before, in a quotation of the penultimate scene of Fellini's *8½*, accompanied by a score of unbearably loud/distorted Musak, he does it literally.

The final scene, under the credits, presents in documentary fashion a group of musicians in rehearsal of a new music piece, doing the real work of changing, fixing, repeating, then packing up their cases—not in silence, but without music—and leaving.

Whale Watching
[unfilmable treatment #17]

I wrote the following two treatments after having seen Whale Watch *by artist Nora Schultz at Vienna's Secession gallery in the summer of 2019 while on tour there with Diana Krall. Much of Schultz's video consists of the sights and sounds of people on a whale-watching boat, observing a patch of open water and waiting for a whale to appear. The video is lovely in its cutting back and forth between ambient wind noise and silence—and clever enough in its use of a fish-eye lens and upside-down camera (the whale's perspective, no doubt).*

But I have to confess that when the long-awaited actual whale surfaces to reward their waiting, I experienced a feeling of deep disappointment.

And I vowed that, in the unlikely event that issues of funding and inertia could be overcome, I would make the following as a corrective.

Consists of a 33⅓-minute videotape of a patch of the Atlantic Ocean taken from a smallish boat somewhere offshore.

There is no land or other boats or people in sight (or at least not in the camera frame).

The sky is overcast.

The season is indeterminate.

The camera is handheld, vérité-style (perhaps you can hear the camera person cough every now and then). Occasionally, the camera may be held upside down, or dangled outside the boat—from the perspective of the water. But there's no fish-eye lens. Whales aren't fish. And there's little reason to believe that either fish or whale would want to look at us in the same way that we look at them.

Maybe the ambient sound of the sea and wind is there sometimes; sometimes not.

The sea isn't too rough, just enough to rock the boat, jiggle the camera a bit.

Occasional cuts/fades to black.

The focus isn't on the distant horizon, but on the forty to seventy-five meters of water just off the bow of the boat. Close enough that you can see the texture of the water.

Occasionally, a bit of the boat itself is within frame. But the point is to really get to know that forty to seventy-five meters of water.

Important: make sure to film in a location in which no whale has ever been sighted.

Sound is recorded live: wind, water, a gull? . . . but no music or dialogue.

Shark Watching: A Series
[unfilmable treatments #18–?]

Modeled after a fun DIY travel show, with a different location every week, and plenty of selfie B-roll documenting getting there, along with clever narration describing the wonders of the place being visited.

On arrival, the narrator/subject/cameraperson/director/producer goes to the beach, puts the camera on a tripod facing the ocean, douses themselves in blood, and gives themselves a small laceration with a razor.

Then, smiling and waving, he or she enters the sea— and waits to be eaten by a shark.

Locations should progress from as far north as it's possible to remain in the water without hypothermia (Halifax?) toward the equator.

> *". . . hope would be hope for the wrong thing."*
> —T.S. Eliot, "East Coker," *Four Quartets*

Bates Airbnb

A remake of Hitchcock's *Psycho*, mixed with a touch of *Who's Afraid of Virginia Woolf?* and a soupçon of *A Street Car Named Desire*.

A young man books a room for four nights via Airbnb. He arrives a bit tired after a day's travel and meets the proprietress, who, although somewhat chatty, shows him what needs to be shown, and then leaves.

He is in New Orleans to look for his girlfriend, who has disappeared after moving there. He has no reason to suspect anything more than that she is sick of him and has found someone new, but has decided, out of an unholy mixture of concern and jealousy, to pursue her.

The next morning at breakfast (organic fruit, Stumptown coffee, local whatever), the yuppie proprietress is chattier still . . . but nothing beyond the bounds of propriety. Her language is absolutely that of contemporary yuppie culture: moved down a few years ago from Brooklyn, knows all the cool restaurants in both locations—they even have some artist or hip band friends in common—contemporary food/restaurant gossip, the obligatory anti-Trump references; all the signifiers of being a well-armed member of the Professional Managerial Class.

In addition, she peppers the conversation with references to her husband Arnold, who she must occasionally attend to in other areas of the house, and her college-age daughter who lives in another state.

However, scary background music reveals that as soon as she closes the door to the guest POV, she's a total psycho, spying on the guest through webcams, and eventually planning to murder him! It is finally revealed, in the penultimate scene, that her daughter was entirely fictional (à la *Who's Afraid of Virginia Woolf?*) and that both the hero's missing girlfriend and the murdered husband are rotting in the basement, dressed up in psychotic college girl regalia—a cheerleader's uniform, a football pennant, a poster of Justin Timberlake. (The music rips off Bernard Herrmann shamelessly and features a swinging work lamp animating the lifeless figures, just like in *Psycho*.)

The last scene features the now obviously deranged and straitjacketed yuppie proprietress talking to herself in the nuthouse, in dialogue stolen from the last scene of *Psycho*—"I just had to tell the police how bad she was. She was always a bad girl. I just couldn't think that I, poor Arnold, would do something like that. I wouldn't even harm a fly"—intercut with Elizabeth Warren campaign material, quotes from the Zagat guide, and material from the Burning Man website.

Throughout, her psychosis is evident in, not in spite of, her yuppie normality.

Part IV

SORRY, WE'RE EXPERIENCING TECHNICAL DIFFICULTIES

The Man Who Didn't Know How
Know How
[tech failure #1]

Once upon a time, in the days before Apple, there was a man who didn't know how to use his cell phone. On a trip to foreign city, he met a woman in a restaurant. They began talking, and soon fell in love. Unfortunately, he had to leave the city that very night. But on his way out, he left the woman his cell phone number, saying: "Call me if you ever travel to my city."

Some time passed, and one day the woman did travel to the man's city. When she arrived, she called him. But the man had turned his ringer off. When he later checked his messages, he heard her voice in his phone saying: "Hi, I'm in town for a few days, and it would be really nice to see you." He could tell she still really liked him because of the shy way her voice sounded.

But that was all she said. She didn't leave a callback number. The man thought there was probably some way to make the cell phone tell him her number—and in fact, there was, but he had lost the instructions. Had he not, he would have known to just push *7, and her number would appear as if by magic. He tried pushing many different but-

177

tons and combinations of buttons, but he never tried *7. The probability is that sooner or later he would have, but unfortunately, he pushed #11+ first, which irretrievably deleted all his messages. And so he didn't call her back.

The woman assumed, after a few days, that this meant he no longer wanted to see her, and eventually went back to her city and never called him again. And so, they never did meet a second time. Which is too bad, because they would have been perfect for each other. They would have married and had a wonderful life together. Instead, each grew old, unfulfilled and miserable in their separate cities, and eventually died.

Once There Was a Man Named Harry Who Couldn't Tie His Shoelaces

O nce there was a man named Harry who couldn't tie his shoelaces. It's not that he was stupid; in other areas Harry had demonstrated keen intelligence and high achievement. In fact, he was employed as a rocket scientist, and had actually designed several rockets. But although tying his shoelaces was not, as people often reminded him, "rocket science," he was simply, for mysterious reasons, unable to do it.

Nor was it the case that Harry didn't care. He knew that with his shoelaces untied, he might trip and break his neck. And if he ever forgot, others quickly reminded him of this risk. It is one of the strange facts of human behavior that the usual social barriers preventing people from addressing complete strangers seem to disappear when the stranger in question has his shoelaces untied. Harry noticed that in this singularly bracketed area of social interaction, the shy become bold, the meek aggressive, and the normally loving full of hate (although, as is often the case, the hate has a pretext of love, the naked anger rationalized by the subject's supposed concern that its untied shoe-wearing object may "trip and break his neck").

Harry had traveled extensively, and noticed that among the infinite variables in cultural norms, the "shoelace exception" appeared to be the one constant. He had even once been advised to tie his shoelaces in a rural area of Senegal by a man who himself wore no shoes.

It was as if the otherwise universal taboo on intimate or aggressive communication with strangers became, in the presence of an untied shoelace, a compulsion, an antitaboo, even among people who wouldn't dream of intervening if Harry had been walking around with, for example, an ax buried in his skull or a syringe hanging out of his arm. The shoelace antitaboo was performed even in places where the citizens were famous for looking discreetly the other way when a child was being molested on the subway, or "not wanting to get involved" when a woman was being knifed to death in a dense residential area.

And so, Harry was often accosted by people tapping him roughly on the shoulder, shaking his arm, or yelling from across the corridor in busy airports:

"Excuse me, but did you know your shoelace is untied?"

"Your shoelace is untied!"

"HEY, YOUR SHOELACE IS UNTIED!"

"TIE YOUR SHOELACE, YOU'LL TRIP AND BREAK YOUR NECK!"

At which point, Harry would try to accommodate his "helpers," even though his own assessment of the risk of tripping before he reached, say, a comfortable seat in the café to which he was headed, was rather low. He would kneel, rather painfully since he had once suffered a torn cartilage, and the prospect of reopening that wound seemed to him more threatening at such moments than tripping and breaking his neck.

But it was no use. Try as he might, and suffer as he did, Harry just couldn't get it right. He could make the tree well enough, and hold it steady between thumb and index finger. And he understood the part where the little snake goes around the tree. But in the next step, where the little badger grabs the little snake and *pulls* it into the hole, something always seemed to go wrong, or was done haphazardly, or without enough conviction . . . so that the knot would come loose after a few minutes of walking.

Harry had learned—or failed to learn—the method of shoelace-tying described above from his father. Harry's father had also been a rocket scientist. In fact, Harry's father was a much better, more famous, and better-paid rocket scientist than Harry, and built much bigger rockets with more geopolitically significant impact. And Harry's father wasn't simply Harry's father: he was also "the father of modern rocket science."

By the time little Harry came of age, however, all the great principles and formulas of rocket science had already been discovered or invented. And besides, even if Harry's ambitions had matched those of his father, and he had sought employment with NASA or the Pentagon instead of a telecommunications network, being "the father of *post*-modern rocket science" wouldn't have had quite the same zing.

It had been a momentary source of some embarrassment within Harry's family, known as they were for mastering much more complex technologies, that young Harry was undone by a simple shoelace. But Harry's father shrugged it off as "one of those things"—and, anyway, he was much too busy and distracted with technologies of state to worry for long.

And as Harry was now fifty-seven and his father had been dead for twenty years, it was too late for him to go back and ask his father what the little badger was doing wrong. But eventually Harry came to observe that in all his years of walking with untied shoelaces, he hadn't even broken his neck once. And the few times he had tripped, it had not been over his shoelace. And he began to quietly reflect on why, given this fact, this singular area of difference should be singled out for public shaming.

Part of Harry's job as a rocket scientist had been the calculation of risk—as his boss at the satellite department of the telecommunications network liked to say: "There's no such thing as a risk-free rocket launch—risk reduction is our mission!"

Harry set to work measuring rates of shoelace tying, comparing them with shoelace-related injury and mortality. He cross-referenced this data with the actuarial tables of major insurers and OSHA studies on workplace safety, and was even able, through an old grad school chum, to get ahold of recently declassified military stats, concluding that in nonmilitary situations, and excluding steel mills and high-rise heavy construction, an untied shoelace was not very dangerous. In fact, Harry found that the statistical probability of untied shoelaces being a cofactor in serious injury or death was somewhere between the risk of installing a pool table in a public drinking establishment, and owning an outdoor grill.

People don't feel entitled to yell, "Get this thing out of here! Don't you know your customers could shoot each other if they lose?" at pool table–owning barkeeps.

They don't shout at people grilling a steak on their roof-deck: "What are you, crazy? It could explode and burn your face off!"

And, OMG, have you read the stats on lighting candles? Romantic? See how romantic you feel when you burn your goddamn house down with all your children inside.

Harry began to feel that there was something irrational—indeed, unjust—about the shoelace antitaboo. And one day, for reasons as mysterious as the lack of lace-tying ability itself, Harry decided he wasn't going to take it anymore. On behalf of himself and people who couldn't or wouldn't tie their shoelaces everywhere, he decided to fight back.

He began by simply ignoring those who commented on his shoelaces, walking past with head held high.

But soon he started to confront his challengers, beginning with a mild "I prefer not to," but gradually working his way up in militancy, from "Untied shoelaces are my conscious choice" to "Your microaggression is offensive: stop it now" to "Off my foot, shoelace-normal pig!"

The fury provoked by Harry's challenge to the privilege of the normally tied was way out of proportion to even his most militant responses. He was beaten, spat on, called the most disgusting names. But Harry marched on, bloodied but unbowed, shoelaces proudly untied.

He vowed to march around the world with untied

shoes . . . He only got as far as Missouri, but by this time had attracted the attention of the news media. Others began to march with him, and he soon found himself the leader of a global movement. He was invited to attend panel discussions with names like "Queer Shoelace Practices," "Shoelace Nonconformity, Race, and Gender: An Intersectional Approach," "Sneakerhead Youth Cultures in Postwar Britain," and "Communities of Shoelace Resistance in the Global Struggle."

Things were going very well, and there was even legislation against "shoelace shaming" pending in Congress. But then an unfortunate thing happened. His former boss's observation about the impossibility of a risk-free rocket launch turned out to also apply to more mundane operations. While en route to the grocery store, Harry tripped on his shoelace, broke his neck, and died.

His obituary in the *New York Times* featured a quote from his neighbor, a Mr. Robert Chaucette: "I told you so."

The Man with the Fun Job

Playing music is fun. At least Dan thought so when he was a kid. He liked it so much he decided he wanted to do it for a living when he grew up. When he told this to his parents, they gave him what they hoped were very stern looks and said, "Well, all right, if that's what you really want to do. But it's a hard life." They said this with an air of authority, because, even though they didn't know any musicians themselves, they had seen a number of biopics on the lives of musicians. In these films, although the musicians did make lots of money and got to do something fun for their job, they all suffered greatly as a result. This worried Dan somewhat, but not enough to make him change his plan. His plan was: 1) Learn singing and guitar playing. 2) Write songs. 3) Start a band. 4) Become famous.

As it happened, Dan was talented, and eventually his life unfolded roughly as he had planned. By the time he was twenty-nine, he had cofounded a band, the Eggbeaters. By the time he was thirty-two, they had a major-label recording contract; and by the time he was thirty-five, one of their records was a college radio hit. Although they never became superfamous like Bruce Springsteen or Madonna or Michael Jackson, they were popular enough to go on tours, and Dan was able to earn a good living playing the kind of music he liked.

Not everything was perfect, of course. Sometimes Dan would have disagreements with other people in the band, or the manager. There were moments when he would feel insecure and wonder whether people would even like the new material he was working on, times when he got tired of touring. But these were all part of what a famous shrink once called "normal unhappiness," and what a normally unhappy person like Dan called "the usual bullshit."

His parents, meanwhile, were still worried. Although their son seemed to be living a very full and creative life, they kept anticipating the inevitable decline into unpopularity and despair, band infighting and breakup, drug addiction, alcoholism, womanizing, bitter divorce, abandoned children, shameful articles in the tabloids, death in complete obscurity, and all the other things that happened to musicians in biopics.

In a way, some of those things happened, but only in the mildest form.

Dan occasionally took drugs and drank, but, being a hard-working type, usually indulged in moderation. Although he tried nearly everything, he was careful to avoid the more addictive substances.

Dan's public, however, enjoyed framing his music within a structure of Romantic Myth. Many fans, and even some journalists, engaged in elaborate fantasies about his drug and alcohol use. If even half of the stories they told had been true, he would never have been able to keep up with his demanding schedule. As it was, only about one-fifth of the stories were true.

Tales of Dan's sexual excess bore a similar ratio of myth to reality. His many rich and varied experiences didn't cause the breakup of his marriage, for the simple reason that they mostly occurred before he was married. Nor did Dan die of consumption or AIDS, although he did once have the misfortune of contracting chlamydia, an experience which caused him to pay more attention to sexual hygiene for the rest of his life.

By the time he met his wife-to-be, Irene, he was a bit tired of fucking around. With two exceptions, one of which caused a terrible argument (and the other of which he never mentioned), he was entirely faithful to his wife for the rest of their long marriage. This was understandable: Irene was beautiful, intelligent, and a songwriter as talented as he was. In addition, she was sexually adventurous and sophisticated, having once been employed as a professional dominatrix. On the whole, even accounting for the cyclical nature of marital relations, Dan's sex life improved greatly during marriage.

The Eggbeaters eventually disagreed on their musical direction and split up after nine successful recordings. But Dan, no longer young by this time, had become somewhat of a "cult figure," due to the eccentric and mildly experimental sound of the early Eggbeaters recordings. He made a number of notable late recordings with younger musicians who were fans of his earlier work, and was now in demand as a producer.

As the years passed, however, critical respect and young

admirers notwithstanding, Dan's record royalties began to show signs of diminishing. Just when this was beginning to threaten the couple's comfortable lifestyle, a major contemporary rock star seeking to demonstrate his knowledge of hip ephemera recorded an old Eggbeaters song on which Dan held the copyright. The song was about surfers, and the recording became a major hit, providing a wave of income large enough to float Dan safely through the rest of an active career, a semiretirement replete with bittersweet reunion tours, and onto the quiet beach of his death.

Now here's the interesting part: just before Dan died, a Hollywood studio asked for the rights to make a biopic of his life. He said okay, but under one condition: that the film not exaggerate his excesses or misfortunes. At first the studio balked, but then Dan actually did die, and the public clamored louder each day for the biopic they felt was their consolation and right.

So the studio gave in. Eventually, they sent Irene a script. Faithful to Dan's wishes, she refused to allow them to exaggerate the drug use or portray it as a tragedy, rewrote the part about the decline into unpopularity and despair, contextualized the womanizing, and crossed out the bitter divorce.

The studio was very angry with Irene. "Nobody will like a movie about a musician who doesn't have these things in them," they told her. But Irene wouldn't budge, and they had no choice, having already signed the contract. *Oh well*, they figured, *we'll make back our money on the original soundtrack.*

Finally, the film was finished. It starred Leonardo DiCaprio, who had spent a whole year learning to play guitar and sing just like Dan, and he did a great job. Sometimes he even sounded better than Dan. Gwyneth Paltrow played Irene. In fact, there was little resemblance, but Irene didn't mind. The outfits were perfect.

What happened at the premiere was very strange. The audience, wildly enthusiastic after the first few musical numbers, seemed to grow increasingly restive as the film progressed. A few people walked out, muttering loudly under their breath. After the film, the audience members gathered in the lobby, trying to make sense of what they had just seen.

"It isn't right," said one.

"It's just disgusting," said another.

"Yeah," said a third, "how come this guy gets to do exactly what he wants his whole life, and have fun and make lots of money, while everybody else either has to do something they hate, which isn't fun, or not make a lot of money, or both? And he doesn't even get punished—instead, he gets to fuck Gwyneth Paltrow! It's no fair!"

"Yeah!" said the crowd, seizing his words. "It's NO FAIR! NO FAIR!"

And chanting these words, slowly at first, then in a fiercely accelerating tornado of rage, the crowd looted the popcorn stand and began to rip apart the kitsch Oriental lobby of the theater.

Irene and the studio execs fled discreetly through a side exit, and were spirited away in a limousine. As they approached the gated offices of their studio lot, they heard the sounds of helicopters, police sirens, and, far in the distance, gunshots.

"Oh my god," said the head of the studio, "I hope this

doesn't happen at the other theaters!" He reached for his cell phone, but it was too late. The producers, fearing a lack of critical support, had chosen to give the biopic simultaneous release in thousands of theaters across the country, and in every single one, the audience had exploded with the same bitter rage.

Back at the cinema, the theatergoers, having tired of smashing the windows, tearing down the marquee, and looting the box office, torched the place before looking for another, picking up intrigued supporters as they ran. As word of the outrage spread through ghetto and commuter suburb, thousands who hadn't even seen the film joined them in support. Inchoate screams of "It's no fair!" echoed through the nation's streets. Eventually, they and others like them burned and destroyed every city in the nation, then went on to burn all the towns. The police and army, sent to arrest them, instead joined in the destruction. They too felt it wasn't fair. Together, they burned almost everything, until there was nothing left. They had the foresight, however, to leave all the Popeyes Louisiana Kitchen establishments untouched. Popeyes is the finest of all fast-food franchises, serving filling and delicious Southern-style chicken, along with New Orleans delicacies like red beans and rice. Even angry theatergoers need something to eat.

When they finished, all the theatergoers and their friends assembled in the ashes of what had once been Washington, DC. Each group elected representatives, and the representatives all got together at a huge event catered by Popeyes, and they immediately passed a new law saying that not only rock stars, but anyone who wanted, could help figure out what to make and how to make it—and make lots of money—just like Dan had done. Feeling that things were now fair, everyone cheered, then went home and rebuilt upon the ashes of society, and lived happily ever after.

Botox
[tech failure #2]

Once there was a man who did something which annoyed his wife. He didn't mean to; it was just an unconscious habit. Whenever he did it she would glower at him with narrowed eyes and furrowed brow, and eventually, he would notice and stop.

As time went on, the lines the wife affected as signs of disapproval became permanent features of her skin. This had two effects: 1) she now had to glower even harder to make the man aware of her discomfort; and 2) she began to dislike her own face, and wish it looked again as it had before the years of glowering.

One day, while reading a magazine, she came across a photo of a woman with creased skin like her own. It was the "before" shot for a skin-straightening product. The "after" shot showed the same woman "look[ing] years younger!" The name of the product was Botox.

The woman quickly called the 800 number in the magazine and arranged to be given Botox herself.

Sure enough, once the initial puffiness dissolved, she did in fact look years younger, and her face took on the pleasant demeanor it once had. Not only were the lines gone, her muscles couldn't form the angry contours if they tried.

But there was a new problem. Now, when her husband did the annoying thing, she had no way to (silently) signal her displeasure. Although in her mind's eye she was glowering as usual, not the slightest ripple of discontent crossed her skin.

So, her husband kept right on doing the annoying thing. She glowered even harder, and her husband's continuing failure to respond struck her as willful insolence and even provocation on his part.

He, of course, noticed nothing, other than a curious discrepancy between a certain tension in her jaw and the placid contentment of her other features.

Finally, unable to stand the annoying thing any longer, she leaped up and beat her husband to death with a frying pan.

She was apprehended for his murder, and executed, fittingly enough, by lethal injection.

The Boy Who Grafted Himself to a Tree

Once there was a boy named Woody who took his name a bit too seriously. When he walked, he walked stiffly, as if he were made of wood. When he talked, his voice sounded like a clarinet. And he was always talking about his lost "roots." Naturally, he wasn't very popular in school, and as time went by, he became very lonely.

Woody didn't like being lonely, but instead of making friends with the other children, Woody decided to try something he'd read about in a horticulture magazine: grafting himself onto a tree.

So, he went out into the forest, searched for the most attractive tree he could find, and held his arm next to a branch. In the horticulture magazine, this approach had worked very well, and the apple and pear trees which had been intimate in this way had gone on to produce whole bushels of little peapples or appears. Woody dreamed of how wonderful it would be to actually become part of a familiar tree. But although he stood valiantly through long days and cold nights, concentrating as hard as he could on merging, his arm and the tree didn't grow together. Nothing happened.

Woody looked at the tree, a handsome poplar, with disappointment and growing disgust. *Why didn't we grow together?* he wondered. *Why, why, why?*

He hadn't wondered very long before he had an original thought: *It's the tree's fault. Must be that poplars aren't good grafters,* he reasoned. And was a good thing too. *Those poplars are so . . . common. That tree just isn't good enough for me.*

So, he set off down the road until he came to a stately oak. He had to climb quite a ways up this majestic tree before he found a branch that seemed suitable for grafting. The height made him a bit dizzy, but he held his arm against the branch as he had done before, with even greater dedication this time, forgoing food, sleep, and many other comforts, and enduring the comments of skeptical birds.

After a very long time, he looked under his arm to see if any grafting had begun. None had. *Oh well*, he sighed. *I guess we weren't meant for each other. Anyway*, he consoled himself, *I could never have been comfortable living at such a height. The stately oak was just a little too . . . stately.* He climbed down and resumed his journey.

By and by, Woody came to a stream. He kneeled down to drink from its water, and when he lifted his head, he realized he was in the shadow of a lovely weeping willow.

A cool breeze from the stream rustled the willow's delicate leaves, which waved gently back and forth as if inviting him into the shelter beneath their branches. The boy hugged the soft bark of the willow trunk. He twined a trailing branch around his arm. He felt at home with the willow. *Surely, this is my tree,* he thought, and began to wait.

* * *

By this time, the boy had been away from his home for twenty-seven days, and his parents were worried. His mother went looking for him all through the woods, shouting his name to the squirrels and chipmunks. His father drove the backstreets downtown asking if anyone had seen a stiff boy with a splintery expression.

They both discovered Woody at once, sitting by the bank of the river with his head in his hands, crying.

When they asked him what the matter was, Woody told them of his sad adventures, of his fears that he would never find the right tree. When he had finished, his mother and father looked at each other knowingly. His mother spoke first.

"Your name isn't really Woody," she told him. "That's just a nickname we gave you when you were very young."

"Really?" he asked. "Is that really true?"

His father came over and placed a hand on his shoulder: "Yes, son, it is. Your real name is Fiorello. It means 'little flower' in Italian."

"Aha!" the boy said, the stiffness already melting out of his limbs, his psychic roots straining against their old container, his clarinet voice cracking into new inflections.

The boy stood smiling between his mother and father.

Yes, he thought. *Of course.* He lifted his face toward the sun. *Fiorello.*

A whole new set of possibilities slowly unfurled before him . . .

For Mauritzio

Once there was a little boy whose parents were assholes. He knew it, they knew it, everybody knew it. But they didn't mind being assholes, and there was nothing anyone else could do.

The boy's parents never had a nice thing to say about him—everything he did or said or made sucked. I'm sure you've read this kind of story before, perhaps in a "human interest section."

But they did do one nice thing: one day, they brought home a puppy. The boy named the puppy Timmy, and loved him profoundly. When the boy's parents beat him, he would cuddle Timmy. The more they belittled him, the more nice things he would say to Timmy; things like "Good dog!" and "Wow, you're really my best friend," which also happened to be true, because the boy and his parents lived at the end of a long, ugly road just outside a dangerous part of an unfortunate city, and no other kids wanted to visit him.

One day, however, the boy stayed at school to play with other kids. He was late getting home, and his parents were even more angry than usual.

In their rage, they did something mean, even by their

standards. They grabbed Timmy, and put him in a box in the car. They said to the boy, "Because you were bad, we are going to give your dog away." And they did. They drove into the center of town, and gave Timmy to a complete stranger who was driving far away and never coming back.

The word "heartbroken" is a cliché. It would have been easier for the boy if his response had been contained in a single torn organ. In fact, his grief at the loss of his dog was indescribable and immeasurable, its pain not containable within his body, or even the world.

When his parents returned, he refused to speak, even though they spoke to, and yelled at, and threatened him. Inwardly, he made a decision that his parents no longer existed. *There is nothing further they can do to me*, he thought. *They're dead.*

And although they did, in fact, try to do many things, none of them mattered to the boy anymore. It was as if he had been granted a superpower enabling him to look through his parents—to erase them. So, in a strange sense, the boy's loss was a liberation.

But it was still a loss. He missed Timmy terribly. It was as if there were a hole in him that could never be filled.

As he grew up, he tried to fill that hole with many things: model airplane construction, reading, radical political commitment, girls, boys, writing, travel, and eventually heroin.

The boy died of an overdose at the age of twenty-seven, in a shabby apartment on East 6th Street, six months to the day after his first publication in a noted poetry journal.

Informed of his death by a neighbor who had read about it in the newspaper, the parents didn't reflect much on how their own behavior might have contributed in some way. "We always said those goddamn drugs would kill him," they told the neighbor, and, satisfied with that narrative, stopped thinking; the magic word "drugs" becoming itself a drug enabling them to treat thoughts of the boy's death as they had always treated thought in general: a kind of filth to be scrubbed away when sanitizing the house.

But as their thoughts about the boy shrank and shrank, something else began to grow in the woods not far from their house.

One day, when walking in those woods, they heard the sound of sticks breaking and branches being torn from trees. They heard a terrible snorting breath, and felt the ground tremble beneath their feet. Suddenly, the trees parted, and the sky in front of them was filled with the form of a huge dog—it was Timmy, grown exponentially and inexplicably larger than human or animal, larger than a house.

This was all so sudden they didn't have time to be frightened in the normal sense, experiencing instead something deeply instinctive, the dispassionate, frozen terror of an insect just before the leaf on which it's been floating goes over the edge of Niagara Falls.

Timmy was bigger than Clifford the Big Red Dog, one of the books the boy had loved reading as a child. Although the new enormous Timmy didn't have Clifford the Big Red Dog's friendly disposition, neither was he vicious or angry. He looked down at the frozen parents dispassionately, impersonal as a tidal wave, indifferent as an earthquake.

He played with them for a while, knocking them about with his enormous paws. When this grew boring, he bit off their arms, and a little while later, one by one, their legs. He knelt on his forepaws, enthusiastically examining his work, enveloping the parents in moist dog breath from his enormous panting tongue. He dragged their truncated bodies down the road by their clothes, and then rolled them playfully up and down some hills. When they seemed to be going to sleep, he woke them by shaking them around in his teeth, the way a fox does a captured rabbit. For a while, he tried seeing how long he could balance them on the branches of tall trees. But eventually, he became annoyed by their piercing screams, and walked away into the forest.

Wilderness
[tech failure #3]

Once there was a man who was tired of big-city life and wanted to spend some time in the wilderness. He went to a camping store and bought all the things he would need for his trip: a tent, a backpack, a sleeping bag—even water purification tablets. He bought a week's supply of food and put it into his backpack. He bought waterproof matches, a compass, cooking utensils, a flashlight, and a map describing how to get to the wilderness. But he was so busy planning his trip, he forgot to charge his cell phone.

When he reached the edge of the wilderness, he parked his car and set off on foot. It was a beautiful day, and before long, the man had hiked so far he could no longer hear any of the sounds of cars or people. That night, he camped out beneath the stars, and cooked the food he'd bought, and had a wonderful time. The next day, he hiked to a desert. He hadn't gone very far before he became tired, and sat down on a rock to rest. This turned out to be a mistake: under the rock was a large poisonous snake that leaped out and bit his ankle. Although it didn't kill him, the poison paralyzed his entire lower body. If his cell phone had been charged, he could have called for help and been rescued. As it was, he lay in great pain for several days.

If only I had charged my cell phone, he thought again and again, before he was finally eaten by a pack of ravenous wild dogs.

Bird

A long time ago I was staying at an expensive hotel in the Austrian Alps. One beautiful day, I decided to rent a bicycle. The courteous concierge told me to select a bike from the dozen or so in the plastic hut used to store recreational equipment. No sooner had I entered than I heard a sound like wings beating against plastic. I looked around but saw only bicycles and badminton sets. Then the whirring sound came again, and on further inspection I saw it came from a tiny bird beating its poor helpless wings against the hut wall behind a radiator. "Poor little thing," I cried, and thought for a moment about stepping on its head. But I didn't. Instead, I approached it very slowly, repeating in a gentle voice, "Don't be afraid, little creature, I'm only going to help you." Eventually, I reached down behind the radiator and took the trembling little body into my cupped hands. "There, there, my friend, what a terrible ordeal you've had today!" I said. Walking out the door of the plastic hut, I flung it into the air, shouting: "Fly free now, little bird! Soar against the wind with the other birds, high up into the sky where you belong." And so it did, chirping merrily as it went on its way. Later that day, I saw a cow.

—Adolph Hitler

Ain't No Sunshine When She's Gone

Ain't no sunshine when she's gone.

But there ain't no sunshine when she's here either.

That's because there simply ain't no sunshine. It's always dark. And that's because of the shadow.

What casts the shadow? It's hard to say for sure.

Some say there used to be a mountain, or perhaps it was a very big tree.

Others say it was all in our head. "We're depressed," they'd say. "Why don't we take Prozac or something?" So we did. But there still wasn't no sunshine.

Anyway, not many remember the mountain or tree or whatever it was. Who knows? The shadow knew: but it forgot.

And now it's nighttime, so the point is moot. She comes, she goes, in the darkness, and nobody ever sees her . . . unless they have a flashlight. Those who do report that she isn't looking well. They say she seems distracted. But what do they know?

Still others place their hope in grammar or Scientology.

The former theorize the double negative as an opening to the possibility that there might have been at least some sunshine (the "ain't no = tis some" theory).

A heretical reading by Triestine radical antipsychiatrists posits a kind of negative sunshine as the cause of the shadow.

(I no, I no, I no, I no, I no, I no . . .)

For Anna, on Anagram Day, 02/02/2020

The Activist (or, Twistin' Time Is Here)

I don't accept ANY aspect of capitalist society. I refuse! I resist! I don't recognize the banks, the military, or the legitimacy of the state! I don't accept my gender, your gender, offenders, Fenders, string benders, or moneylenders.

I reject all raced constructions of color, horse, human, or rat. I don't accept the choices on offer at the supermarkets, the bodegas, Trader Joe's, Walmart, or any so-called alternatives thereof. I don't accept my shoes. I don't accept my age, my hair, my weight, my breath, my face. I don't accept my language, my religion, or my death. I vote no! I break consensus! I refuse! I resist!

I don't accept the lesser of two evils, or the greater evil, or the greater good, or the lesser good, or the greater lessness, or the evil good good evil live dog god anagram Anaheim Heimlich maneuver spamarrest cardiac mammogram anodyne or any other possibilities or impossibilities hereunder hereafter whatever whereas wherefore whereunto unto which therefore herefore for hear two ear dog faced et cetera.

And I put this in the form of a proposal to the committee: why and wherefore how to whereas I motion object veto this table and table this emoticon.

Other items I do not accept include but are not limited to: shoehorns, sperm, razors, and giraffes. I don't accept sidewalks, I walk on my hands in heavy traffic, and even that is a compromise. I don't accept gravity—or teeth! I don't accept you or what the mainstream media refers to as your cute little (and I quote) "doggie."

And furthermore: I don't accept Donald Trump (no, I don't mean his politics: I mean his eyebrow, his kidneys, one of his earlobes, his birthday party, his alphabet, the god who created him, the world he farts in, or any other worlds that happen to be in the vicinity or remote distance).

It's all been polluted, disgusted, erupted, disfigured, dismembered, forgotten, encrusted, interpopulated, miscegenated, impregnated, bifurcated, frustrated, menstruated, lacerated, and macerated.

And that's not all.

It's also been: masturbated persecuted evolved disfruited tutti-fruttied highfalutin digested invested protested and registered in the flat-chested Westchester Best Western festering pest of a percolating mink collector.

I refuse, I resist. I wash my fecal mouth with soap. I inject fentanyl into my eyelids. I pluck my balls out with a runcible chopstick. And I demand the immediate resolution of ALL contingencies!

I don't accept Jesus, Jehovah, Allah, Satan, or my mother's cunt. I spit it all out. Ptui! Toi Toi Toi. Caw caw caw. Oy Oy Oy. I refuse, I resist. I refuse, I resist. I refuse, I resist. I refuse, I resist!

I don't accept e-flat minor, trichords, major 3rds, perfect 5ths, or any note above the barline. I don't accept boxed ears hook noses split lips black eyes or any features below the hairline. I don't accept hooks lines sinkers or crabs on either side of the waterline.

I've had it. I'm done. I'm finished. I'm going on strike, and from this time backward will agree to a common language on CONDITION that the word NO is excluded from your vocabulary absolutely and permanently without exception or absolution. YES! YOU CAN SAY: YES YES YES! (You can also say "affirmative," or "jawohl," "yes sir," or "ooh la la.") And whereupon furthermore, as specified in the articles of submission, Section 2, Letter B, Clause 5 Subsection E, I will shit in my pants WHENEVER and WHEREVER I want, and when I am tired, or for any other reason unable, unwilling, or disinclined to walk, you will CARRY ME wherever I need to go. YOU WILL PUSH ME ON SWINGS and you will LIKE IT. You will sing me to sleep until you puke and read me stories until your eyes deflate. YOU of all people will sign your name on the dotted line or I will have you fed to invertebrates. And when I am sick I will vomit. And when I am sad I will laugh. And when I'm fat I will roll down any hill I want rolly rolly rolly rolly all the livelong day in the twilight's last gleaming round midnight and in the blue of noon. I will force myself on a calculator. I will sweat into my personal incubator. Until, on the command of three . . .

The red spotlight explodes and I crawl back up the hole from whence I came to be or not to be sustained forever and ever floating in a sac of amino paradise hooked up and booked up until the worms that buried the pyramids all crawl home and the radiant pharmacologists return to bury their parasites.

O altitude. O decrepitude. O sisters of the heavenly

mantra: call me back into the void, call me back from this shitty clapper. Call me out of this body this city this endless performance of aching plaster. O numb nurse mother turn off my drip. I won't refuse, I can't resist. *Another world's possible!* Only not for us. *Arise ye prisoners!* But not tonight. *Let's do the Twist like we did last year!* Only not for us, and not tonight, and certainly . . .

Not here.

(It's late, the meeting's over, we motion to adjourn. Someone volunteers to fold the chairs and post the minutes. Outside the sleeping city, the current gathers force against its embankment.)

for Lynne Tillman

Once there was a kid who lived in a house.
He shouldn't have lived in a house: he should have lived in an apartment.

But others—his parents—made him.

He went to school. But it was the wrong school.

On the test, he gave the wrong answers.

That's why he went to an inferior college, and learned the wrong things.

Afterward, he couldn't get a good job; he had to get a bad job.

He did it badly, and the things he made all broke.

Everyone was angry; they asked for their money back. He didn't give it to them.

He went home to his house. It was an ugly house, on the wrong side of the tracks.

There was a better house on the other side of a fence. But there was no gate in the fence.

His roommates were always home. They were stupid people. They didn't know how to drive cars. And when computers were invented, they didn't know how to use them, either. They all got the wrong kind of computer—the kind nobody used anymore. They couldn't figure it out. The screen froze. Everything they had written was erased; it didn't matter because it was all wrong anyway.

Somebody important told him: if you had a girlfriend, you wouldn't be wasting your life. So he got one . . . but not the one he wanted. He had wanted the one next to her. He should have asked that one out, but didn't. So she went away and lived happily ever after with someone who was richer, smarter, better looking, and had a bigger dick. And he married the wrong one.

It wasn't a happy marriage.

When things broke around the house, he couldn't fix them like a real man, even though there were tutorials online explaining everything to everyone, meaning that anyone who couldn't do anything was stupid.

They went out to a restaurant; but it was the wrong one. Everyone on people-supposed-to-know.com said the one across town was much better. But they didn't know. When they got there, they ordered the wrong thing. It tasted like shit, but they ate it anyway. Then they went home and had bad sex. Neither of them came.

Somehow, she became pregnant anyway.

The baby was ugly and cried incessantly, night and day. They couldn't stand it, so they went to the store and bought a book: *How to Make Babies Stop Crying* by A Famous Doctor, who, a few years later, was revealed to be a quack. The book advised them to put the baby in a soundproof box until it shut up.

It worked, but the baby grew up to be a monster who liked to torture animals, bit the other children at the playground, and peed in his pants until he was seventeen.

"We've created a monster," they said to each other within hearing distance of the monster/child, again and again.

They went back to the store and bought a much better book, which described how to be "good enough mothers." But it was too late.

The worst thing, from their perspective, was that now all the parents whose children shared their toys, and didn't bite or spit on or rub dirt in the eyes of the other children, could all see that they weren't "good enough."

This was upsetting to them so they went to a psychiatrist who told them that their perspective was all wrong: the fact that their child was unhappy should have bothered them more than what the other parents thought. The fact that he knew this about them, while they barely knew anything about him, proved that he was much smarter, so they agreed. And why would they have gone to a doctor if they hadn't been sick, anyway?

But the monster/child didn't actually seem unhappy. He spent every waking moment that he wasn't physically forced to do something else playing online video games in which he seemed to derive a great deal of pleasure from shooting, stabbing, punching, kicking, bombing, dismembering, or incinerating his opponents.

They made the mistake of asking a neighbor's advice. "He'll probably grow out of it," the neighbor said.

He didn't. The monster/child—now a monster/teenager—ceased all communication with his parents beyond grunts and shrieks when forced away from his video game. He was failing in high school and had no friends other than those whose avatars he bludgeoned online.

But in a way, the neighbor turned out to be right.

Some of the monster/teenager's video comrades started a chat group in which they imagined how much more fun it would be if they could do things IRL that they had been preparing for in their games. The comrades (who were all white males, heterosexual in aspiration, if not in actual practice) decided that doing these things to racial minorities, women, and homosexuals would be the most fun.

Someone in the chat group made some money as a YouTuber, and one day, the monster/teenager told his parents he was leaving. He put his clothes and laptop in a plastic bag, and got into a black van with his comrades—none of whom he had ever met before IRL—with the intention of driving to rural South Carolina, taking whatever menial jobs they could find, and beginning weapons training on the weekends with a white supremacist militia.

He didn't turn to wave goodbye.

Although this wasn't what they'd hoped for, the parents realized that they were to blame.

Eventually, they forgot about him.

When the great plague hit, the man was fired from his job.

On the way out, one of his colleagues gave him a tip: "Buy Zoom stock. Everybody's going to be using Zoom in the plague." But the man was too stupid to listen.

Later, the former colleague and he recognized one another from behind their face masks in the Costco checkout line. The former colleague said: "You should have listened to me, Charlie. If you'd invested your $1,000 severance check, you'd have ten thousand dollars right now."

The man's name was Charlie.

Acknowledgments

Enormous thanks to Kurt Hollander for making this publication possible, and to Sydell Rabin for planting the seeds.

Grateful acknowledgment is made for permission to reprint some of the pieces in this collection:

"Lies and Distortion" first appeared as "Earplugs" in *Arcana: Musicians on Music*, edited by John Zorn (New York: Granary, 2000).

"Guitars" was originally published in *State of the Axe: Guitar Masters in Photographs and Words*, edited by Ralph Gibson (Houston: Museum of Fine Arts, 2008).

The interview in "Frantz Casseus" was commissioned by and first published in *BOMB* No. 82, Winter 2003. ©*Bomb Magazine*, New Art Publications, and its Contributors. All rights reserved. The *BOMB* Digital Archive can be viewed at www.bombmagazine.org.

The interview in "Robert Quine" was commissioned by and first published in *BOMB* No. 89, Fall 2004. ©*Bomb*

"The Attack on Artists' Rights . . . and Me" was originally published in an earlier form in *Talkhouse* (October 11, 2014).

"Still Things That Move: The Poetry of Henry Grimes" appeared in an earlier form as the introduction to *Signs Along the Road: Poems* by Henry Grimes (Cologne, Germany: buddy's knife jazzedition, 2008).

"Songs of Resistance" originally appeared as liner notes to the eponymous album.

"Playing Hal Willner Home" was originally published as "Amacord Hal Willner" in *All About Jazz* (April 15, 2020).

"The Twenty-Three-Day Tour" was originally edited by Kurt Hollander and published in *Sampling the City: The Portable Lower East Side* 11, no. 1, 1994.